Suddenly, something snapped inside my head, and I rushed blindly forward, hands reaching for the throat of the seated man. With one tremendous effort, I lifted him bodily out of the chair and held him above my head, where his arms and legs waved madly, like a beetle on a pin. With one grasp on his throat and the other around a leg, I swung him back for an instant, then threw him half the length of the room. Out of the corner of one eye, I could see the sergeant trying to tug his pistol from the holster, and I smacked him alongside the head with the flat of one big hand, knocking him sprawling to the floor.

A rifle went off in my ear. . . .

ROBERT BELL
To The Death

BALLANTINE BOOKS • NEW YORK

Library of Congress Catalog Card Number: 84-90940

ISBN 0-345-31937-0

Manufactured in the United States of America

First Edition: December 1984

This novel is dedicated to my friend Charles Leland Hill, a researcher and collector of our country's historical past. Where a lesser man would long since have surrendered to what most considered inevitable, he has shown me the true meaning of courage, and his faith and loyalty remain an inspiration. Mr. Hill has been a paraplegic for twenty-seven years.

Author's Note

Discrimination did not exist at the defense of the Alamo, and had no influence on how or when a man might be killed; nor did it rear its ugly head on March 27, 1836, a day when 342 survivors of the Battle of Goliad were massacred by gunfire, sword, and bayonet. Included among those men who died defending the Alamo were the Mexican-American-Texans Juan Abamillo, Juan A. Badillo, Carlos Espalier, Gregorio Esparza, Antonio Fuentes, and Andres Nava—all from San Antonio; and Galba Fuqua, from Gonzáles.

Truly, many races and creeds were joined in founding the great state of Texas! We now believe the word *Texas* came from the Indian name *Texia,* denoting a confederacy of some tribes in the eastern portion of the state. Early Spaniards used *Tejas,* meaning "allies" or "friends." In native-born Texans runs the blood of the English, German, French, and all the nationalities of the world. Whites, blacks, the red men, and the Oriental—all did their share in carving out a great state, but the first colonists bore Spanish names.

Robert Vaughn Bell
Creek Park Ranch
September 1983

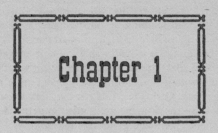

Chapter 1

Wellsir, I reckon the whole ruckus started when a mouse-colored horse come limping through the corral gate at Rancho Montoncillo. What we call a grulla down here in the border country—a slate-gray gelding. Plumb wore out and streaked with lather, he was dying on his feet; but what he was packing on his back was already long dead.

It was long about midday and I'd been just poking along toward a wide place in the road called Juno when I decided to drop in on our neighbor Don Carlos Montoncillo, who owned one of the biggest cattle spreads in southwest Texas. Me and my big buckskin was feeling the need of some shade, even though it was still early summer; and we were figgering on a pull at the stock tank for Buck, and mebbe a long, tall drink of something cool for me. Besides, if I was lucky I might just get a chance to talk with Esperanza, though it was coming on to siesta time, and more'n likely she'd be napping in her room. Carlos seldom taken advantage of the siestas, but I knew that his beautiful daughter followed the old customs.

Me 'n Buck were coming up on the gate—a massive, two-part affair with a crossbar up high, formed out of a squared-off tree truck. Dangling on chains was a thick bronze shield with the Montoncillo coat of arms on it, and above it was fastened an old cow skull, with its long horns reaching out more'n four feet in both directions. Carlos had told me the story about this particular critter. Seems how his great-great grandpa Golondrina, on his ma's side, had been given this big grant of land by the king of Spain and had used this beef critter as a lead steer when he drove his herds up from Old Mexico.

More'n once that critter had pulled him out of some real tight spots, one time when the herd balked on fording a fast-moving river; and so he never could find the heart to butcher him. That big steer lived to be over thirty, and he finally died of old age.

As I reached down and unlatched the gate I seen a rider coming way off to the south. Wasn't moving fast enough to even raise any dust, so I reckoned it to be one of the don's vaqueros. Rate he was ambling along it'd take him an hour before he made it to headquarters.

Old Buck whickered over that way, but it was too far off for the other horse to hear. I walked him through, fastened the gate, and loped on down the tree-lined road. Ahead, the ranch buildings loomed up, looking more like one of them old castles you read about in the history books. A high tower at each corner of the fortlike quadrangle rose up at least thirty feet, and each one held a vaquero with a rifle. The front was the actual home of the don and his family—a two-story structure with wide balconies by each window—while a pair of long, low adobe bunkhouses formed two parallel sides of the rectangular fortress. Corrals and a hay barn enclosed the fourth side, all made from thick adobe blocks.

One of the sentries must have spotted me, because a middle-aged Negro man was waiting by the open doors, and a vaquero accepted my reins and led old Buck around in back.

Them doors was something else, I want to tell you. Oak-planked and brassbound, they reached up about twelve feet and had to be four inches thick. I walked on through, waited a moment while the servant closed the door, then followed him across a tile-floored entry hall. It was huge, with a pool about ten feet across in the center. Water ran out of a pitcher held in the hand of a life-sized marble statue of a young girl, and green plants were all around. My durned spurs were making a racket, so I bent down and taken 'em off before following him through an arch into the patio.

Don Carlos was sitting way back in a far corner in a big chair that looked like a throne. He looked up, smiling.

"Buenos días, my young friend. What brings you to Rancho Montoncillo this early in the day?" He pointed toward one of the four chairs. "Come, sit down. Would you like to have some coffee, or would you rather have something that is cold? A rum drink, perhaps, with some lemon and ice."

"I'm purty dry," I told him as I somewhat gingerly settled my bulk in that chair. When you're packing three hundred pounds on a six-ten frame, like I am, you learn to be careful whereabouts you sit. "I b'lieve somethin' cold *would* help," I said. "If it ain't too much trouble, that is."

A *mozo,* one of the many servants around the ranch, seemed to come out of nowhere, and Carlos pointed to his glass and held up two fingers. *"Y bien fría,"* he cautioned.

A scrawny youngster was squatting in the shadows, in back of Carlos's chair, with a brass-framed Winchester carbine in his lap. One cocked eye was staring at a point somewheres over my left shoulder; then his good eye flickered briefly in an unmistakable wink as I lifted a hand in greeting and spoke.

"Qué tal, Poco Luce? How've you been gittin' along?"

His over-wide mouth stretched in a gap-toothed grin that threatened to split his pockmarked face, and he grunted some unintelligible greeting. *Poco Luce,* meaning "Little Light" in Spanish, was sort of a slang expression for somebody with a bad eye, like his. Besides having that cocked eye he was also a mute, and he got his meanings across with grunts and his own variety of sign language. Devoted to Don Carlos, he was his constant shadow, pantherlike, and a real demon with the carbine or a knife. Despite an inclination toward gauntness, he was the strongest little devil I'd ever seen for his size. Why, he could lift the husky, six-foot don on or off his horse and pack him in his arms for short distances, like to a chair.

You see, Carlos had been crippled more'n twenty years. A vengeful woman, the wife of a renegade rancher, had shot him in the back after he killed her husband in a fair gunfight. Her bullet had cut the spinal cord and left Carlos paralyzed from the waist down, but he'd refused to let that bother him. So he'd designed a special saddle, fitted with straps to hold him in place, and continued to oversee the workings and supervise the hands on the half-million-acre rancho.

Poco Luce made few friends. Aside from his master, the little feller really cared for no one. But for some strange reason he'd taken to me right off. Why, I couldn't guess, but he'd always shown a fondness for me. As for his feeling for Carlos, that dated back to when he was just a younker.

Seems Carlos and his men had come up on some Comanches in time to save the boy and his mother. Poco Luce's pa had already been killed, and the Indians were trying to drag off the two of 'em when Carlos rode in. Ever since, he'd shown this doglike devotion, and would die to save his *patrón*.

The servant showed up about that time and set our frosty glasses on the table. I lifted mine gratefully and let about half of it trickle down my throat.

"Ummm," I murmured. "Thet sure enough hits the spot! You gotta excuse my manners, Carlos. I was dryer'n an old bone, and this was the medicine I needed."

He smiled and sipped at his drink. "Tell me," he said. "Do you have a particular reason for stopping by? How is everything coming along at your new ranch? Any news of Rush? A letter, perhaps, or maybe someone who has seen him?"

"No, sir, nary a word. Leastways, not since old man Simms come back from Abilene with the story 'bout Rush dealin' in cattle over to Kansas City. Ma wrote to some feller last month—a yard boss at the stockyards. But we ain't had any answer up to now.

"Far as me droppin' by," I went on with a grin, "I jest figgered it'd be a good idea. 'Sides, it's purty hot, and I needed coolin' off. By the way, how's Miss Esperanza these days? She used to ride over now and then, but I ain't seen her now for a month of Sundays."

Carlos smiled. "Why, she is just fine, Lysander, but a child has been ill. The daughter of my *segundo,* Sanchez. A serious illness that has required medical care. Esperanza, as you know, had some training for such things at the Academy for Girls in Brownsville, and so she has been constantly at the child's bedside. Fortunately there has been much improvement, and Esperanza will be free to ride again. Now she is enjoying the siesta, but I will send a servant there if you wish to see her."

"Nah, thanks anyway, Carlos. I'm glad to hear the little girl is gonna be all right, and I'm sure Miss Esperanza will ride over our way one day soon. Well! Lookee here, now! Look who's passin' up his siesta! Miguel Vargas, top hand on this here rancho, and my old sidekick."

I stood up as the foreman neared, and stuck out my hand in greeting. Vargas stepped back playfully. "Aiee! No! I value my fingers, little brother," he said with a grimace of pain, hiding his right hand behind him.

"The last time I shook your hand," he went on, "it was a week before I could handle a riata properly. You are just too damn strong, *compadre.* Better I have my hand in a bear trap than to trust it to your grip. Once is enough!" Both Carlos and I laughed at the foreman's wry expression, and Vargas joined in as he pulled a chair over to the table and sat down.

"What brings you here to Rancho Montoncillo? Is there no work for you to do at your new place?" He leaned forward a bit and looked at me real serious. "Have you heard from your brother Rush? Does he know you have located on grass, in both your names? Now is when you need him, with that new ranch and only two hired hands."

"I don't know, Miguel," I told him. "I've written a letter, and so has our maw, but we haven't heard a word. Mailed the letters in care of thet buyer—the one we sold cattle to when we got to Abilene. We've heard from the buyer, but nary a word from old Rush. I guess we—''

Suddenly an alarm bell in one of the towers began its dull clanging, and we heard a vaquero shouting something about a dead man on a horse.

"Ay! Peligro! Peligro! Vengan todos! Yo lo veo, seguro! Miran al hombre muerto montando a caballo!"

I stood up, and that's when I watched that grulla limping through the corral gate. Plumb wore out, he stopped next to a stock tank and stood there spraddle-legged, his head hung down, and muscles jerking and twitching in his flanks. Like I said, the horse was dying, but that feller on his back had already cashed in his chips.

Whoever had done it had lashed together a couple of mesquite branches in the shape of an X. This was rigged behind the cantle, and the dead man was tied upright with some rawhide strips. They'd shot him to doll rags, and it'd been done while he was on the horse, because his blood had soaked the horse's back and run down his legs. More'n likely the poor critter had run himself into the ground trying to lose that scary thing on his back.

Vaqueros were pouring out of the bunkhouses, and me 'n' old Miguel was only a step or two in front of them. Up closer it was even worse. His shirt was ripped mostly off, and we could see raw, red patches on that poor feller's back. The devils had cut strips off him and used them to tie him up!

A dozen vaqueros were swarming around that horse, and I'd never heard cussing like that anywhere. 'Course it was most all in Mexican, and I'd already found out it was possible to say a lot more in that language. Then Don Carlos hollered, and he wanted to know who it was.

"Quién es ese hombre, en caballo alla? Es él uno vaquero de miyo? Digame, ahorita! Tell me, right now!"

"Momento, patron!" Miguel looked over at me, and his expression was a sick one. He reached up and taken a hold of the dead man's hair, tilting the head back and looking into those

dead eyes. For a long moment he just stared; then he shuddered and let the man's head down gently.

"It is Sosteno Aragon, *patrón,* one of our riders, but the horse is that of another man. I believe this grulla belongs to Vincente Moreno." He turned to one of the vaqueros, then called out, "*Sí, patrón.* It *is* the horse of Moreno." He looked the gelding over carefully, reaching down and touching the swollen knees. The grulla was breathing hard, rasping like the sound of tearing cloth, and blood showed in his nostrils. He was wind-broke, and suffering.

"*Gracias,* Miguel," Don Carlos replied. "As a favor, cut the man loose and have some men carry his poor body over to his *jacal.* Better you go along and explain to his wife that I will come and speak with her very soon. Then return here, as a favor, so we may discuss this affair and make plans to avenge this dishonor. *Siga!* Hurry along, and return quickly. That man, Moreno, may be lying out there wounded!"

"Immediately, *patrón!* Don Carlos, this poor beast can no longer survive. With your permission, I will see that it is spared any further suffering."

Carlos nodded, and as soon as the dead man had been taken down and the saddle and bridle removed, that grulla fell to the ground, a bullet in its brain.

I stood there while two other vaqueros backed a team up to the dead animal and then dragged it away. The bloodied, bullet-scarred saddle lay there on the ground with blanket and bridle flung over it, and I got to looking.

Many Mexican saddles are works of art, and this was purely one of 'em. Ours were really just copies of theirs, as they'd been at this business lots longer than we had, but I reckon we run to plainer stuff—more for doing the job than pleasing the eye. My own was one of them Mother Hubbards, a saddle built on pretty much the same tree as the Mexican's, with a big, flat horn and the cinch rigging passed over the pommel and cantle and down to a full, double rig. What was called a *mochila,* a loose leather covering, fitted over the whole shebang and made it some comfortable to ride.

Whoever had made Aragon's must have spent a lot of time,

and he was an artist for sure. Deeply carved in a flowered pattern, with solid iron stirrups laid over with copper horse heads and coiled rattlesnakes, it was an outfit a man could be right proud of. A machete like a short sword was hung over the horn in a carved leather scabbard. Now, that just didn't make any sense.

If the Comanches had done this thing, it was a hidebound cinch they wouldn't have passed up a saddle like this. Some buck would have grabbed it right off and sent the dead man home sitting on a blanket. Plus, that machete was a weapon to be feared, and Indians ain't inclined to be plumb idiots. They might leave a fortune in money laying around, 'cause the stuff ain't much use to them, but they never left weapons.

Vargas came back about then and told Carlos he'd delivered the message. "The *esposa* of Sosteno Aragon will have a child soon. It will be their first," he said, staring at the ground and shaking his head sadly.

Carlos nodded. "We must make certain that she lacks no comfort," he said. "But first, this wrong done to one of us must be avenged. Tell me. Where did Aragon and Moreno work today? How many others did you send along? Do you think this is the work of *indios?*"

"Comanches!" the foreman replied bitterly. "It is of no use to warn these youngsters. I told them to make sure that one man was always watching, but these young men will not listen. It's a game with them, this chasing of cattle from out of the thorny thickets. These idiots even keep score, and when one of them has less than another, then he will literally risk his life for more."

"I sent Sosteno with three other vaqueros to clear out the cattle hiding in the brush along the river. Especially to round up some old dry cows we can no longer use for our brood stock. These will go along on the next drive, together with the four- and five-year-old steers, but Sosteno won't be going. Not this year. Not ever again."

"*Es imperativo, patrón! Con permiso,* I will take along a fighting force, and we will track these devils to their village and leave not one human being alive. They must all be killed, so that *indios* everywhere will walk wide around a rancho such as this one.''

Don Carlos nodded, but his forehead was wrinkled in serious thought. Then he looked up. ''Why have these Comanches sent Aragon here as they did? To gain what? Another thing is bothering me. The Comanche always takes the scalp, and yet Aragon still has his hair. I've been told that for the Comanches the taking of a scalp is more significant than a killing. A dead man's spirit may come back to haunt the one who killed him, but without his hair, the killer is powerless. This seems to be some sort of symbol, but of what? They wouldn't be warning us to leave the ranch. Not after all these years have passed. Think of it! One hundred fifty years! No! I don't believe the Comanches have done this thing. Maybe, we have someone who wants us to *think* the Comanches are guilty of this horrible crime. But why?''

I had to get my oar in, mainly because I agreed with him, but also because I figgered stirring up Comanches could only lead to more trouble.

''Listen, Miguel,'' I said. ''Let's not be runnin' off half-cocked, as the sayin' goes. Sure, we got to find them men you got out there and help 'em all we can, but let's not be raidin' Comanche villages until we're sure of our ground.

''Another thing. Thet saddle of Aragon's would've looked mighty good on some Comanche's war-horse, and I doubt that they'd leave a fancy machete. I agree with your boss. Mebbe somebody *wants* us to think the Comanches killed Aragon. For what reason, I ain't got the faintest, but I got me a hunch we're gonna find out, and we may not like the answer.''

Vargas looked at me hard, then he nodded to Carlos. ''*Sí, patrón.* I understand; but we must go and look for the other vaqueros. So, with your permission, I will do that now, if it is your pleasure.'' He faced around.

''*Atendeme,* Sanchez! I want ten mounted men, and I mean right now! They are to carry Winchesters and the revolvers that shoot six times. Food for three days, and corn for the horses. You are to stay, Sanchez. As *segundo,* you are boss of those I leave here to protect our *patrón. Asi, oiga con cuidado!* Take care! Riders must be sent to warn all of the men at the line camps. Tell them what has happened, and to be alert for attack at any time.

"I know this does not leave many here at the rancho, but this must be done. Arm the servants. Give them Winchesters to use, because they are not skilled in the use of firearms and will need the breechloaders. There are more than enough to go around." He paused, then went on.

"One more thing. Find Sēnor Gilkie, *el cocinero negro,* the black cook. He is a *veterano* of many battles and will be your second-in-command. Tell him I said this thing."

He turned to Don Carlos. "We must go now, *patrón.* With your permission. Sanchez is a good man, and you have Poco Luce, *el mudo,* who is always by your side." He backed away, then turned and ran toward the corral.

Rising from my chair, I gave a hitch to my pistol belt, a gift from Miguel Vargas, and reached for my hat. "I'm gonna trail along with 'em," I told him. "No tellin' what they're gonna find out there, and I ain't lookin' forward to more'n what we've already seen; but if them Comanches *are* figgerin' to raid south, my folks might be in real trouble. Like Mike said, Sanchez is a good man, and Lancelot Gilkie is sure enough bad medicine when it comes to fightin' gun battles. I seen him in action, and he's meaner'n a one-man army. You 'n' Miss Esperanza will be plenty safe right here."

"I understand, Lysander." Don Carlos shifted his crippled body in the chair. "Ride carefully, and stay close to my men until you have full knowledge of what has happened. We will be perfectly safe here at the *estancia.* Like your own home, this one is built to withstand a siege. So! *Vaya con El Señor,* my young friend, and come back safely."

We shook hands, and I turned toward the corral. I could see old Buck tossing his head and prancing around, like the noisy confusion was no mystery to him. He was all rested up now and raring to go. He sidled toward me when I reached for the latigo so's to tighten the cinch and durn near put me on my back when my spurs crossed and I stumbled.

"Doggone you, Buck. Big as I am, you outweigh me by

most four times, and you ain't no ballerina. Now, knock off
thet shovin', and give me a chance to fix this riggin'!''

Wouldn't you know he curled up his lip and showed me them
big, yellow teeth, like he was grinning, and let go the noisiest
whistle you ever did hear. Sounded more like some old mule
than a Kentucky Standardbred, which was what Buck and the
rest of his kin really made out to be.

You see, brother Milo's new wife, Julia, had brought them
horses into our family just last year, and us being fairly good-
sized fellers, we'd welcomed these big critters. Texas horses,
being's they were mostly mustangs, are real small in size; wiry
and tough as heck, but not tall enough to keep my feet from
dragging. So when Julia and her grandpa, Eliakim Sprague,
showed up with this cavvy of fine horseflesh, I was even more
tickled than my two brothers. We . . . Aw, heck! That's another story altogether, and chances are you've already heard all
about it.

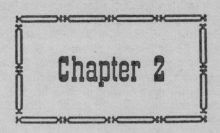

Chapter 2

Not knowing how long this ride might be, I taken the time to dry Buck's back, and I smoothed out the blanket before replacing the saddle. Vargas showed me a wooden box near one of the gateposts.

"Cartridges for the Winchester," he said. "Take all that you can carry, amigo, for we have no idea what we will find, backtrailing this *caballo*. Also, make sure your *olla* is not leaking, and the water inside is fresh. Rations, and grains for the animals, will be carried on packhorses, but you must carry your own drinking water."

I nodded as I taken up the flank cinch. I'd filled my canteen before leaving our place, so the water'd mebbe be a mite warm, but it was still full. My saddlebags only held a spare shirt and some socks, so I had plenty of room to pack ammunition. I could use more than the others, because I had two revolvers that could gulp down as much as the carbines.

Most fellers during this time still carried the old cap and ball revolvers, because that's all you could buy. Me, I had a pair of .44 Remingtons that had been converted to use the Henry rimfire cartridges, the same ones that fit the new Winchester rifles.

Frank Curry, who ran a harness shop in the nearby town of Juno, was a fair to middlin' gunsmith, and he'd done the job for me. Everyone on the frontier was familiar with guns in them days, but I taken more than the usual interest. I hung around old Frank's shop whenever I had the chance, and liked to help out when he'd let me. Most times it was only a spell at pumping his foot-powered lathe, or drill press, but I got a real thrill out of watching them chips of steel curl up and drop in the pan. I envied Frank his knowledge.

One day a feller came in with a busted Colt, and it shot the Henry cartridges. He'd had some Mexican gunsmith do the work, and it was pretty crude, but it shot fine. Right now it was just a broken spring that needed replacing, and Frank got that done in a few minutes.

After the man left, I asked Frank if he'd fix one up like that for me, and he'd agreed. Wound up, I had him convert a pair of them, using the solid-frame Remingtons that we both knew were more dependable than the open-top Colts.

Frank figgered the easiest way to do the job was to make complete new cylinders, and that's what he'd done. I'd had him cut the barrel down on one of them, and I carried it in a special rig under my left arm. A loading slot was cut in the right side of the recoil shield, and the hammer needed a slight alteration, but the cap and ball cylinder could still be used in either gun. I carried a loaded and capped cylinder in each shirt pocket, just in case; also a short twig to punch out the fired shells, because there was no ejector rod on the guns.

The cartridges came fifty to the box, so I scooped up ten boxes for each saddlebag. That gave me a thousand rounds, and

I figgered that'd last through an average-sized war. We might be outnumbered, but we'd let 'em know they'd been in a fight. Right now I didn't know who "they" might be, but we would soon find out.

Vargas's instructions had been given in Spanish, but this was no problem for me. Three years along the Mexican border had given me a fair working knowledge of their language, so I could palaver pretty good. Matter of fact, I'd found that a feller could get a lot more said in Spanish, and I wasn't near as backward in talking as I was in plain old *Yanqui*.

It looked like Vargas and his vaqueros were ready to set out, so I made a last-minute check to make sure nothing was being left behind. A flurry of activity on the far side of the corral caught my eye. The knot of riders was moving out, and hats were coming off as they bowed their heads for a slim figure on a leggy chestnut horse headed my way. I wrapped my reins around a corral rail and waited there for a moment, then reached up to help her down. Even with the protection of the Spanish lingo, I still stammered when the words of greeting came out. She was so durn beautiful, with the scent of fresh spring flowers in her hair.

"Shhhh," she murmured as she placed a finger on my lips. "Slowly, my dear friend, else how am I to understand thee?"

Despite my helpless confusion, I smiled and stepped back a pace, still holding one of her hands in my own. The words *thee* and *thou* were natural when you were speaking to an equal or to a loved one, but they still sorta threw me. We *were* just friends, although I gotta confess I had a lot more than just friendship on my mind.

Esperanza was six years older'n me, me being only twenty, but that made no difference in my feelings. What did count was the fact that she'd been raised by a wealthy father and I'd come from a side-hill farm in Kentucky. We'd never been without food, 'cause we raised all we ate, but I'd wore hand-me-downs from my two older brothers until I'd got bigger'n either of 'em and Maw had to make me my own. Not that them brothers of mine was little fellers. Milo stood six-six, with shoulders to match, and Rush was just a couple inches shorter. Even our maw topped the six-foot mark.

Esperanza was tall and willowy, just like my maw, and her flat-crowned red hat was on a level with my chin. Her hair was blue-black, and drawn back in a knot, which let the fine bones of her cheeks show clear, while the gold flecks in her hazel eyes glinted from behind long, black lashes.

Red suede *chaparejos* formed a protective covering for her black, divided riding skirt, and a full, deep bosom swelled, unconfined, behind the embroidered front of her white linen shirtwaist as she pivoted, a slight blush coloring an ivory complexion that seemed to mock the rays of the Texas sun.

"Did thou plan to leave without at least saying good-bye, señor? Have I done something to offend thee, or . . ." A grin showed perfect white teeth. "Or has thou found someone a bit more beautiful, and perhaps more understanding?"

I glanced all around us. At least nobody was close by to witness my confusion. This was not the first time she'd left me all mixed up. Twice I'd come to the ranch fully intending to propose marriage, but couldn't find the words.

"There never will be another for me, Miss Esperanza." The words came out slow and deliberate as I puzzled for more to say. A shout from Vargas told me it was time to ride out.

"I gotta go now," I told her. "But I'll be back soon. You think on what I jest told you. I ain't much on speakin' fancy words, but I know how I feel about you. I know you're the onliest girl in the world for me, and I want you for my wife. I ain't said nothin' to your pa, but I think he must have guessed by now. So you study on it, and I'll be back here soon for your answer. There! I've said it!"

Her blush deepened, and she leaned closer, her lips parting slightly. Them eyes looked long and searching into my own, and she tightened her hold on my hand.

"In English," she said, "Esperanza means 'hope' and 'expectation,' and I *have* hoped, and I *have* yearned with expectation. I've waited, Lysander. Waited past the age when most girls marry. Waited for the right man. I've known you were that man since the night we first met. The night that you came to my father's *baile*. You can have my answer now, but I'm sure you can see it in my eyes."

Vargas let out another bellow, impatient to be on the way out, so I had to get going. Some of the vaqueros tried to conceal their grins but weren't very successful. Gently, I disengaged her hand and swung up on the buckskin.

"I'll be back," I told her, reining Buck around. "And we can talk to your pa. Meanwhile, you take care. Stay close to the home place and you'll be safe."

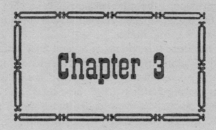

Chapter 3

Some two hours later we found them three boys lying down around the foot of a cutbank next to Devil's River. It was buzzards circling overhead that led us to the spot, but even then none of us were really prepared for what was waiting in the mud of the nearly dry stream.

One youngster had a big old cow caught by her hind feet, and his rope tied fast to the horn. All of 'em were dead—the cow, the horses, and the three vaqueros—all sprawled in bloody heaps, with the green death flies clustered on them. It was pretty awful, the way they'd been shot up and hacked with knives and left to lie in the blood-splashed mud.

A crude attempt had been made to scalp one of them, but I

was sure now that this was the work of white men. When an Indian takes the scalp, it is done cleanly, much like a good surgeon would do. A semicircular cut is made just above one ear, and the knife is run in under the skin far enough that a grip can be taken. Then, stepping on the victim's face with one foot, a quick jerk rips loose the entire scalp, and another swift cut leaves it in the Indian's hand. This must be done in battle most times, and speed is important.

Whoever had done this had made several false starts, then finally wound up taking only part of the hair. Knowing that Comanches usually taken all they could get, I figgered white men, for whatever reason, had butchered these boys.

While some of our vaqueros loaded those pitiful bodies on the spare packhorses, me 'n' Miguel scouted around. The sign was plentiful, and the way it looked there'd been no chance for the boys to fight back. The shooting had been done from on top of the bank, and they'd been like sheep in a pen. We found fired shell casings scattered in the grass, and they'd come from Spencer rifles, or carbines.

None of the sign showed shod horses, but that didn't mean it was Indians that killed them. Lots of fellers don't put shoes on their horses, because in this sandy soil it wasn't necessary. But I noticed them marks showed hoofs in healthy condition, like they'd been trimmed regularly. Then, off to one side, I found a pile of fresh horse droppings with some oat grains scattered through them and what looked like cut hay stems. One thing sure, that horse hadn't had to forage for his feed. At least not recently.

A shout from Miguel made me look up, and I saw him waving something in the air and motioning me to come over and take a look at what he'd found. The blood scent had the buckskin dancing and sidestepping nervously, and when I pricked him with a spurred heel he humped his back and came unglued.

Feeling some depressed myself, I'd just started to roll a smoke, and he caught me unawares. Next thing I knowed, he'd dumped me on the ground and was on his way home.

With a whoop, Vargas and most of the vaqueros taken off after him and left me lying there feeling the fool. I sat up and taken my pouch out again and dusted some grains of tobacco into the paper, twisting it into a cigarette. Looking through my pockets, I found I didn't have me a match, so I just laid back down and studied the sky.

Them buzzards were still circling, high up, and I thought about trying a shot at 'em with one of the Remingtons. But I changed my mind. After all, that *was* their job, and the good Lord put 'em on earth to keep it cleaned up. Still, as I lay there thinking about it, I couldn't help but feel just a little sickened at the sight of 'em. A shiver ran down my back when I got to thinking about them tearing at what used to be folks. I knew they were supposed to wait until a man was dead, but I wondered. Supposing they were really hungry? Supposing they'd gone for days without a thing to put in their bellies? Mebbe a feller was *almost* dead, and mebbe he'd even started to stink from his wounds. Would them old buzzards still stick to the rules? Would they wait until he was for sure dead and gone? Or would they just dive right in and start tearing chunks off him?

I got to thinking about a time last year when we'd buried some fellers that brother Rush had killed. They'd shot a lot of holes in my other brother, Milo, and was sneaking toward the house to finish us all when old Rush reared up in front of 'em and started blasting away with a sawed-off.

He'd killed four men and their horses, and when we taken a wagon out there next morning the buzzards weren't even a little bit bashful. Matter of fact, they'd acted like we had no business there at all. We'd had to beat 'em off with our shovels. After we loaded the dead men in the wagon, I taken the team and dragged them dead horses up next to a cutbank, much like the one here by the river. Then I caved the whole thing over them horses. When we left, them old buzzards had landed on the dirt pile and was trying hard to dig 'em up.

Old Rush was sorta like a father to me. Paw passed away when I was just twelve years old and left a big blank spot in our lives. Milo was seventeen then, and Rush was more'n two years older'n him, so he taken charge. Course Maw was a strong-minded woman, and she did most of her mourning by her lone self, though she did sorta lean on Rush for a while.

Then the war come along, and Rush 'n' Milo signed up with a bunch called Vaughan's Brigade. They rode off, and me 'n' Maw didn't see 'em again till the war was over. Wasn't much of anything left on our place, 'cause foragers from both armies had picked us pretty clean. Jeff Davis let the boys hang on to their horses, so they brought them home, along with guns and other things they'd picked up on battlefields.

We put together a wagon and headed for Texas, where we'd heard land was there for the taking. Found us a fine place, right along Devil's River, and bordering on Beaver Lake. My brother Milo was married now and busy ramrodding the home ranch, while I had located on a new place for myself and my other brother, Rush.

Right now Rush was somewhere in Kansas or Missouri, and we hadn't seen nor heard from him for almost a year. One of our neighbors, coming back from a drive to Abilene, heard he was dealing in livestock in Kansas City but couldn't get an address. I sure missed him. Rush was an organizer. One of them fellers that gets things done, if you know what I mean. He was never afraid to talk, and when he did, what he had to say always made sense. Folks believed in Rush and followed him when he had a plan and set out to do it.

Our paw had been like that. A big man, almost a half a foot taller'n me, Paw was a full-blood Choctaw Indian whose folks had all been chiefs in the old days. His Indian name being hard to pronounce, he taken Maw's proper name, and was called Ebit McCowan. When some folks looked down on Maw for marrying an Indian, she told 'em Paw was the only man in the county she could look up to, and it was more than him being tall that she meant by that. Paw was a leader. If he'd not died before the war got going, he'd've been made a general or some such, just like old Stand Watie, the Cherokee.

Lying there on my back, I could feel vibrations and hear the noisy vaqueros coming back with my horse. The cheerful-sounding yelps were at odds with the way I knew they must be feeling, and yet this was normal for men like us. The enormity of what had happened would take a while to sink in, and when it did, tempers would rage and these killings would be avenged ten times over.

With my horse Miguel handed me a metal button almost as big as a silver dollar. A wire band on the back was hanging loose by one end, and the face had a wreath border enclosing an embossed horse's head.

"It's a rosette off of somebody's bridle," I said, giving it back to him. "Don't b'lieve I've ever seen one jest like it. Doesn't look like it's been out here very long, so the chances are it was lost by one of the killers. Hang on to it for a while. Mebbe we'll come across its mate."

Vargas nodded and slipped it into his shirt pocket. "We can send one of the vaqueros back with the bodies," he said. "The way these tracks lead out, they're heading toward that line camp at Indian's Draw. If they mean to hit that camp, chances are we'll be too late to be of any help. Not more'n four hours from here, and I would say these tracks are five or six hours old. Whatever they've intended to do there I would imagine has been done. There are only four vaqueros and an old Chinee cook at Indian's Draw, and they would not have a chance against these backshooting killers."

I taken out my bowie and marked an X in the dirt. "I figger we're about right here," I said. "And Injun's Draw's over here." I made another mark. Reaching over, I thrust the knife into the ground, making the three points about the same distance apart.

"This here's Sycamore Canyon camp. Now the way it looks to me, these killers seem to know their way around the ranch boundaries, and chances are they'll be headin' over toward Sycamore Canyon after they git their dirty business done at Injun's Draw. Both them line camps are around the same distance from here, so why don't we hustle on over to the other camp and set up an ambush for them killers? Like you said, we're too late to help the one bunch, but we can sure enough make them killers wish they was never borned."

Quickly, the sorry business of tying the bodies onto pack-horses was accomplished and the one vaquero detached as the leader. Miguel gave him a written message to Carlos, with a full account of what we'd found and where we were headed.

The three dead horses and the cow were left unburied, a reminder of a senseless slaughter, and we rode on out.

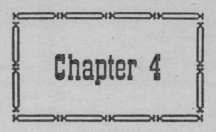

Chapter 4

The sun was low on the horizon, when we rode into one end of Sycamore Canyon. I'd been here several times, and I knew the camp was about midway along the north side and facing a view of the Blue Hills. This was no thrown-together outfit, with ramshackle brush shacks, or *jacales,* as we called them. Instead, a small adobe ranch house with a roomy bedroom to house Carlos on his frequent visits stood next to a lengthy bunkhouse that held beds for a dozen riders. Two barns and a combination cookshack-washhouse made up the rest, together with big cottonwood corrals for horses and cattle.

Right now, dust rising above one of the corrals meant the vaqueros' day was still going strong. Can see to can't see was the general rule on Texas ranches, and this one was sure no exception. As we got further into the canyon, two riders broke away from the corral and headed toward us. A moment later I recognized one as being Luis Marindo, who had taken the trail to Abilene with us last year. He was riding that same fine-looking chestnut he'd set so much store by, so's I remembered the horse before I did the rider. His partner was a real stringbean, thin to the point of emaciation, sitting a flashy liver bay with a light mane and tail.

"Hey! Gringo!" Luis hollered when he got close enough so's he could recognize me. "I know ju! How ju been? We don' see ju fer long time. Say, ju come here jus' in time, amigo. We got damn *buen caballo* fer ju to ride. How ju lak show these feller wha' ju kin do, eh?"

Suddenly he realized that nobody was smiling. His big grin faded, and he shot a look at Miguel Vargas.

"*Qué pasa contigo, Caporal?* Why are you here with these men so heavily armed? Are you looking for the Comanches? I don't see any *indios* for a long time now."

In a few terse sentences Vargas explained what we'd had waiting for us alongside the river. Also about the tracks we'd seen and what we figgered the killers would do next.

"Come!" he ordered. "Let's tell the others. We may have little time to prepare for the attack, and I want to be sure we get every last one of these murderers."

"Let's try and keep one of 'em alive," I told him. "Your boss will be wantin' to know why they did this and who hired them." Vargas nodded, and we taken off for the corral.

A rider was just picking himself out of the dirt when we got there, while another, mounted man tried to catch the bay horse that'd bucked him off, a wild-eyed gelding that must have had some ideas of his own. About the time the cowboy had himself brushed off, the fool horse come running at him, and he barely rolled under the fence rail in time. Laughing at his scowling face, I helped him to his feet.

"*Alguna vez es mejor por agarrar la comadre,*" I told him; meaning that sometimes it's better to grab the horn, no matter if the other boys do laugh at you—even necessary, if you figger on riding that horse to a standstill.

The vaquero started to snarl something, then taken a closer look. "By all the saints," he yelled. "It's Lightly! How is your health, little brother? I've been stuck here in this forsaken canyon for six months now and wondered if we would ever see each other again." He threw out his arms in mock astonishment. "You're still as big as a buffalo," he said. "Tell me, does your mother still set the full table?"

I nodded, grinning at him. "Fuller'n ever, Paco," I told him. "The latchstring's always out to our friends. My maw loves a big eater, and she allus figgered you for one of the best plate polishers in West Texas."

Paco Quintan had also been along on the drive last year, as had the other man, Emilio Fernandez, and we'd become good friends. My folks had hung that name "Lightly" on me back before I grew to grizzly size, and most everybody around our place still used it. I was christened Lysander McCowan, but that was a mighty weighty name for a youngster. 'Sides, I'd never much cared for it, and liked Lightly better.

Quick-like I explained why we were there. "Me 'n' you'll git up on the canyon wall, Paco." I pointed to a ledge that was directly above the ranch house. "You'll need to bring your Winchester, but I got cartridges enough for both of us. We'd best hide these horses in one of the barns, but leave a few out in plain sight. Chances are these hombres know that there's jest five of you working here, and I figger we'll be facin' a reg'lar charge, jest like the cavalry. They'll try to rush in here and git it over with real quick, so's they won't have to waste time starvin' you out."

The ranch house, along with the cookshack and one of the barns, backed up to the canyon wall, while the bunkhouse and the other barn extended to the front, with a horse corral off to one side. Vargas was already stationing men in the lofts of both barns and on the roofs of the two dwellings. Both the bunkhouse and the ranch house had thick adobe parapets along the front edge of the roofs, where the vigas, or rafter poles, protruded. By chipping around the top of the vigas, a man could have himself a dandy firing port and still remain well protected. Looking over to one side I saw the cook, a fat one-legged half-Apache named Santos, heaping sacks of corn behind an open window of the cookshack, then lying down behind the stack with an old musket and a double shotgun.

I led Buck into the back barn, tied him in a stall, and gave him a couple of forks of hay to keep his attention. Then me 'n' Paco got ready to climb the canyon face. I brought my saddlebags with the twenty boxes of cartridges and my own brass-framed Winchester hung over one shoulder with an improvised sling. Miguel Vargas met us at the barn door, and with him was Luis Marindo and his skinny partner, Flaco.

"I'm sending Luis and Flaco out to scout both ends of the canyon," he told us. "Soon as they see that bunch is coming in, they'll ride here fast. They'll both be in a position where they can see each other, so one of them won't get left behind when the bunch is spotted. We have to keep the boys acting normal, so Fernandez and Montoya will be working some horses in the corral.

"When the killers come in sight, the two of them will run to the bunkhouse, hollering real loud. This shouldn't raise any suspicions, and should lure them in." He paused. "We are going to shoot them down like dogs," he said. "There'll be no warning, and no quarter given, except for the leader." Again he paused, and looked at our faces. "I want him to know why he is dying," he told us. "I want him to crawl, to whimper, and to scream for mercy. No one is to shoot at the leader. Is that understood?"

We all nodded, and me 'n' Paco headed toward the back side of the ranch house. Being much lighter than me, and mebbe a bit more agile, Paco reached the ledge first and offered me a hand up. It was a perfect spot. Running water had eroded a narrow cleft along the canyon wall that was perhaps three feet deep. Room enough for both of us to be completely hidden from view. We were at least sixty feet above the canyon floor, behind a natural fort of solid rock where not even a ricochet could get at us. All we had to do was wait.

Wouldn't you know, after being so careful in my plans, I had forgotten to bring along my canteen. Right away that was all I could think about. I taken a squint over at Paco, but no canteen was in sight. About the time I'd decided the climb down would be worth it, Paco hissed at me and motioned me to get down.

Dropping to my knees, I glanced down canyon and saw both our riders racing in toward the ranch buildings, and not far behind, a massed bunch of horsebackers, coming fast. It looked like there were at least twenty of them.

The sun was down behind the rim now, and shadows reached out along the canyon. The light would hold for mebbe twenty minutes, but it gets dark fast when you're hemmed in by the walls of a deep canyon like this one. C'mon, boys, I whispered to myself. C'mon! Let's get this over with!

I taken out both my Remingtons and thumbed in a sixth round for each cylinder, then laid them on the ledge out in front of me. Jacking the action partially open on my rifle, I made sure there was a cartridge in the chamber and watched Paco do the same. I'd decided to use my revolvers first, because the targets would be in close. Time enough to use a rifle if some of them survived the first barrage and tried to escape on horseback.

Luis and Flaco came thundering into the ranch yard, making a flying dismount near the corrals, and they were only a few steps behind Fernandez and Montoya, who were running toward the bunkhouse, hollering at the top of their lungs. About two hundred yards back rode the leaders of the outlaw pack, brandishing rifles and closing fast.

I guess I'd had it on my mind from the beginning. The business of shooting these fellers down without giving them warning stuck in my craw. I knew they deserved no quarter, after murdering them boys like they'd done, but this wasn't my style, and I just couldn't do it. I doubted I would have many friends among the vaqueros present, and they might decide to turn their guns on me. Vargas might understand, but he'd be mighty angry and unforgiving. No matter. I had to follow my conscience or I'd never rest easy again.

The only way to warn them would be to fire a round in the air and call on them to surrender. With all the noise and confusion they might not even hear me, but I had to try. I got ready. When the front riders reached the corral, that would be the time for me to fire that warning shot.

Suddenly, a puff of powder smoke blossomed in the open hay door of the far barn, a revolver boomed, and the clear voice of Miguel Vargas carried across the ranch yard.

"Stop! You are all surrounded and have no chance! Throw down your guns and raise your hands in the air or you will all die! *Alto! Echan por tierra todos sus armas!*"

God bless Miguel Vargas! He'd got me off the hook, and I would never forget it. I should have known he couldn't kill anybody without giving them a chance.

Down below, everything was confusion. The leading riders had hauled up, and those behind were crashing into them. A few raised their guns and fired toward the barn, and the resulting fusillade from our vaqueros cut into them like one of them scythes cuts down waist-high grain. Most of them in the front crashed to the ground, and horses struggled to get up as their riders cursed and screamed in pure terror.

A few of the riders fought to get clear of the tangled mess and charged toward the ranch house, waving rifles and firing in all directions. They were met with a regular broadside from at least six rifles firing from atop the roof, and all of them were swept off their horses and fell to the ground.

Now that they'd opened the ball, I felt right about doing all the shooting I could. Me 'n' Paco both were firing at whatever targets presented themselves, and I'd scored twice; that I was sure of. One feller on a big sorrel horse was wheeling around down there, and I could hear him cursing and hollering at the others. He was a big man, with what looked like some kind of uniform coat, and boots up over his knees.

"Fall back! Fall back!" he was shouting. "Find cover, or we're all dead men!" He had his reins wrapped around one of his arms, and a revolver in each hand.

I figgered he had to be one of the leaders, only with the way things were going, he'd have nobody left to command. As I watched, he taken aim at one vaquero, standing up in a hay door and firing point-blank into the churning mass of horses and men struggling below him.

I'd shot them Remingtons empty and was punching out fired cases with my stick and thumbing live cartridges back in both guns. Before I could grab up my rifle, the big man had touched off his pistols, and the luckless vaquero pitched to the ground below. Remembering what we'd decided about saving a man to question, I deliberately held high and put one round into his shoulder, knocking him back off his horse.

The mixture of powder smoke and coming nightfall made them fellers hard to see, so's mostly we were firing at movement. I had no idea how we were faring, but I knew the killers had to be hurting. A lot of them screams we heard were hollers for mercy, and I figgered they'd about had their fill.

Vargas must have been thinking the same, because he began shouting out, *"Desistan sus fuego!* Stop the shooting! Hold your fire, hombres! *Lo eso bastante, pero tienen cuidado!"*

Almost immediately the shooting stopped, which I figgered meant we were doing most of it. There were a couple more shots fired, then complete silence, except for the groans of the wounded men and the terrified sounds of injured horses.

"Bring some lanterns from the bunkhouse," ordered Vargas. "Be careful now. Some of these men may be playing dead, so don't take chances. Kill any man with a gun in his hand."

Paco was already scrambling down the canyon wall, and I'd finished loading the Remingtons and stuffed them back where they belonged. Slinging the rifle over my shoulder, I taken the saddlebags in one hand and started sliding behind Paco, hoping my heavy leather chaps would keep me from losing too much of my hide. Dark as it was, the handholds were hard to see, and with mebbe ten feet to go, I plumb ran out of luck and fell the rest of the way down, taking Paco with me.

"Chihuahua!" he exclaimed, as we both sat up and made an attempt to get untangled. "Thy weight is like that of a fat steer ready for market. Next time warn a man before trying to crush him!" Neither one of us was hurt, and it taken just a moment for us to get to our feet.

I choked down the laughter that threatened to break out and told him to watch his step. "Keep close to the wall," I warned him. "That way we blend in with these rocks and we make a poorer target. I doubt all them fellers are hit bad, and I don't want to lose you now thet the shootin's over.''

Lanterns were bobbing and swinging, and a circle of light was converging on the downed men and horses. I could hear a chorus of moans and curses, and more than one plea for mercy was cried out. Vargas continued to warn everyone to take no chances and to shoot anybody who resisted.

A terrified horse charged the circle, and a man wailed in fear as he fell from the horse's back, a foot caught in one stirrup. ''Oh, Gawd! Help me, somebody!'' he screamed as he swept past us, his arms flailing and his body bounding along.

I made a grab at the headstall as they reached us, but I was hampered by the heavy saddlebags and missed. A choked, blubbering scream came from the helpless man, then they were out of sight in the darkness. A moment later the screaming stopped, but the sounds of the galloping horse continued.

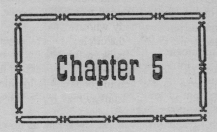

Chapter 5

Once we had enough light to see by, we taken a full count of the dead and wounded. Surprisingly, we found five of the invaders who weren't even scratched. With all them bullets flying around, you'd have figgered nobody could escape being hit at least once.

Some were stunned and just lay there, helpless, as angry vaqueros menaced them with cocked Winchesters. I reckon the surprise had been complete. After shooting down hardworking buckaroos like a bunch of corraled sheep, a show of resistance had been the last thing they'd expected. Chances were they'd slaughtered the boys at Indian's Draw, who would have had no reason to suspect these killers were on the prowl.

Two of Vargas's men were collecting some guns that'd been dropped and were searching for others that might be hidden; and they were none too gentle as they ripped shirts open and roughly rolled a man over to check his back pockets. One of these, who'd not been touched by a bullet, was fairly young and scared plumb out of his wits. He was sobbing, and his shoulders shook.

As a husky vaquero bent over him, a glittering knife held in one hand, he moaned, "Please! Don't kill me! I ain't never done you no harm! We was just follerin' orders." The vaquero drew back in disgust. An acrid odor and the damp, spreading stain on the front of the cowering man's pants were shameful proof of his overpowering fear.

That feller I'd shot off the horse was sitting up now, a look of hate on his bearded face. "If you mean to kill us," he gritted out, "then do it and be damned to you! I ain't going to crawl, no matter what. You!" he spit at me. "What are you doing here? You sure don't look like no greasy Mex! Are you gonna stand there and let these men treat us like a bunch of animals? We're white men, just like you!"

"You'd best keep thet mouth shut," I told him. "No *white* man would ever do what you 'n' these hired hands of yours did to those boys by the river. If I had my way you'd all decorate the nearest tree. Right now we'd like to know why in hell you had to murder them poor vaqueros. They was doin' a job of work, and they wasn't harmin' you none. You see your way clear to tellin' us who's behind all this, and there's a slim chance you might jest save thet hide of your'n."

He laughed. "Why, you lily-livered Mex lover, you! You think I'm gonna tell you anything, you got you another think coming! G'wan! Do your damnedest, but I warn you, mister, a mountain's gonna fall on you! You and these dirty Mexicans of yours. You're gonna wish you'd never been borned!"

"Enough talk!" Vargas was keyed up pretty tight. "We've done enough talking," he went on. "And I've heard all these threats about what might happen if we don't turn you loose. Now we're going to hold court on you men and select proper punishment for this terrible crime you have committed. Take them to that barn there. Be sure they are tied tightly, so that none can escape. If any man gives you trouble, shoot a bullet into his belly and let him bleed to death.''

He turned to me. "Bring a lantern, *compadre,* and we'll check the headstalls on their horses. If we can find one of those horsehead rosettes like the one I picked up, then the proof will be conclusive. They did the shooting by the bank of Devil's River, and they must pay for their crime.''

A vaquero handed me one, and we began inspecting the gunmen's mounts. Six had been killed, and the others were held by two of the vaqueros. "How'd we make out?" I asked. "Did we lose many? I saw one shot down by the bearded feller. A youngster who was up there in the hay door. I reckoned the boy was a goner, the way he went all limp and fell from out of that doorway. Do you know? Was that boy killed?''

Vargas nodded. "Yes,'' he said soberly. "It was Nerio Lucero. He just turned eighteen last week. A good boy, or rather, a good man. If he was old enough to die, then surely we could call him a man. We were lucky, Lysander. Nerio Lucero was our only casualty. A few others suffered wounds, but they are minor and will not keep any man from doing his job. These youngsters are tough, and used to being hurt.''

"What are you gonna do with these men?" I asked. "How do you figger to punish them? We ain't the law, Miguel, and we ain't got no jail to hold them in, nor can we be both judge and the jury too. How're you fixin' to handle thet?''

Vargas turned. His voice was low-pitched and serious. "The soldiers have left Camp Hudson. All that is left there now are a few enlisted men with a sergeant in command. We cannot depend on them to punish these men, and I doubt that we could even persuade them to lock the men up.''

"There is the deputy U.S. marshal, of course, but he's no friend to Texans. Chances are he would arrest us for even daring to fight them. So we will do what has to be done, and take the responsibility for our actions. You can understand, can't you, *compadre?* When there is no law officer, a citizen must uphold the laws of the land, or soon we'll have anarchy—

lawlessness and disorder that will make a mockery, a travesty, of what was done by those who settled Texas.

"We used to have a Ranger force, and lawbreakers respected them. They dispensed justice on the spot, and when a man was obviously guilty, he paid the price. Now we have these soldiers from the North trying to 'reconstruct' Texas. They know nothing of the problems we face here, or if they do, it is easier and safer for them to look the other way. There are some among them who see this as an opportunity to build their fortunes, and they make their own laws, counting on an indifferent federal government that's over a thousand miles from Texas and cares little for ex-rebels."

To tell the truth, I was some surprised to hear all this coming from Miguel, who was just a foreman on a cow ranch, a hired hand who worked for another man. 'Course, I knew that he'd had some education. Carlos's pa had sent Vargas clean to Mexico City back when he was just a youngster. Sent him there to study law. Something to do with a promise he had made to Miguel's pa, who'd been with the family for all his life, and served them faithfully until he was killed.

Seems Miguel hadn't taken kindly to schooling, and those professors had seen that right off. So they'd sent him on back to the ranch. 'Course, old man Montoncillo had been put out, but he'd let the boy work as a vaquero and gave him an opportunity to work up to foreman.

He wasn't no youngster, 'cause he'd been working before my friend Carlos was even born. I figgered he had to be close to seventy, but you'd never know it. Strong as a bull, he'd keep a feller humping just to stay up with him.

While all this talking was going on we'd been looking at the outlaws' horses, and we found the twin to the rosette on a big sorrel horse. Miguel spotted it and asked me to let him have the lantern.

He fished the one out of his shirt pocket and held it up close to the other. "You see, amigo, it is exactly alike! Whoever rode this horse helped to do that killing at Devil's River. There's no doubt of that."

The horse *was* a sorrel, and it sure did look like the one the bearded feller had been on when I'd shot him. I wanted to make sure before I committed myself, so I taken the lantern and looked over the rest of the horses. There was one reddish bay, but he had a black mane and tail. None of them others came close to being a sorrel, so I spoke my piece.

"The feller thet done all the talkin' was ridin' a horse thet was a dead ringer for this 'un," I told him. "I knocked him off the horse when I shot him in the shoulder, so there ain't no mistake. I reckon thet puts him in the bunch thet done the killin's, all right, less'n this is somebody else's horse and he's borrowed it." I leaned forward and taken a closer look.

"Lookee here, Miguel! There, tied on thet saddle string! Thet's hair, ain't it? It's a scalp, and it's still bloody! Why, he must be the hombre thet scalped poor Aragon!"

Vargas stepped closer as I held the lantern high, and he cursed under his breath. Shaking his head, he reached up to his forehead with his right hand, then down and over his chest, as he made the sign of the cross and murmured words that I couldn't catch. Stepping back, he motioned for me to follow, and led the way to the barn.

Inside we found the prisoners sitting close-huddled on the dirt floor, ringed by the armed vaqueros. The one who'd seemed to be the leader was silent now and apparently in a great deal of pain from his wounded shoulder. The rest were apathetic, except for the young one who'd shamed himself.

Tears had left dirty streaks down his cheeks, and a deep, shuddering sigh escaped as he saw us enter the barn. Since I obviously was not a Mexican, perhaps he thought of me as a possible savior, because he tried awkwardly to struggle to his feet and get my attention. The vaqueros had used ropes to hobble them all, in addition to tying their hands, and he fell heavily on his face in the dirt.

Rolling over, he stared wildly at the ring of grim men, who fingered their rifles as they glared back at him. "You gotta help me!" he shrieked. "They mean to kill us all, and I don't wanna die! I didn't kill nobody. Honest! They made me come along, but all I did was hold the horses. Find that gun of mine. You'll see it ain't been fired! Please! I—"

A blue-rimmed hole suddenly appeared in the middle of his forehead, and a dull boom echoed in the cavernous barn as a ring of dirty white smoke rose from the derringer pistol in the bearded man's hand. The youth's head jerked back, and a moan came from his lips as he slumped to the floor.

Quick-like I leaped forward and wrenched the pistol from the killer's hand as he fell back with a groan. It was one of them all-metal single-shots made by Moore that used .41 rimfire cartridges. A little gun with a big, heavy bullet, it had killed the boy instantly.

Despite his efforts to kick me, I rolled the bearded feller over and found a slick little holster cleverly sewn on the inside of his belt, in the hollow of his back. Somehow he had managed to get the pistol out and fire it, even with his hands tied behind his back. Now, them things were sometimes sold in pairs, so with that in mind I looked a little further. In his left boot I found another holster and a mate to the first gun. In his right boot was a long sheath that held a double-edged dagger and four leather loops in which extra cartridges for the derringers were held.

"Well," I told him, "you're a regular walkin' arsenal." I handed the knife to Miguel and stuffed the tiny derringer in a vest pocket after first checking to see that it held a cartridge. Loading the second gun, I looked around the circle and spotted Marindo. "Here, Luis," I said as I tossed him the derringer. "This might jest come in handy sometime or other. Put it where you can git at it easy-like."

He grinned and tucked it away in a chap's pocket. "Hey! *Gracias*, gringo! Ju are lucky feller, ju know. Thees guy he look for keel ju, but ju take hees gon, an' hees knife. Now hees gonna be plenty sorry, ju bet, 'cause these boys an' me, we gonna put rope roun' hees neck, an' hees gonna go *gaaahhh . . .*" With one fist up behind his ear, his eyes rolled up and his tongue lolling out of one corner of his mouth, he pantomimed a strangling man.

Several of the other vaqueros joined in, making the same gurgling sound and twisting their faces into grotesque and comical masks. One already held a rawhide rope, and he made a noose in one end, then tossed it over one of the hand-hewn beams overhead and jiggled it suggestively.

I had no real idea as to what Vargas had planned for the invaders, but I figgered this had gone far enough. "Let's cut out the comedy, fellers," I said. "This here is serious business, and men's lives are at stake. I'm all for hangin' 'em, but let's lay off the jokes. There's more'n one way to torture a man, and I jest don't believe in any of 'em." The vaquero with the rope pulled it down and began coiling it up, while the others quit their grisly shenanigans.

I taken Vargas to one side. "Like I said, Miguel, whatever you have in mind, I'll go for it. If you want to hoist these fellers up right here and now, I'll help pull on them ropes. But I figger that Don Carlos is really the one best qualified to pass judgment on 'em. I never got to join the army, like my two brothers, but I know there's a thing about the chain of command. You work for Don Carlos; this here is *his* land, and them was *his* men that got killed. There ain't a bit of doubt that these men did the killin' and they are guilty as hell, but I figger the final word rests with him."

He nodded. "I feel the same," he told me. "I know the *patrón* trusts me to make the right decision, but this is far more than I want to accept." He shook his head. "To hang twelve men, no matter how much they deserve to die . . . It is too much. No, we will guard them here tonight and travel in the early-morning hours.

"One more thing," he went on. "Would you check and see how badly their wounded need treatment? I know that the one you shot must still have that bullet in his shoulder. This should come out even if he hangs tomorrow. I won't let any animal suffer, and I can't feel differently about these men. We have some medicine and bandages on one of the packhorses, and I'll have one of the men get it out. We'll need to take care of our own wounded also, although none are hurt badly. Can you do this thing for me, *compadre?*"

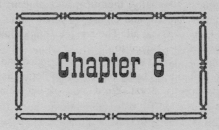

Chapter 6

Sun comes up about five at this time of year, but we had been on the trail for half an hour by then. I'd've bet hard money that past night would've been a sleepless, wide-awake one for me, but seems like I'd no more'n leaned back when blessed, dreamless sleep came to me.

I'd made Vargas promise to wake me around midnight so we could each take our turn in guarding the prisoners. Neither of us figgered they would give us any trouble, what with the vaqueros just waiting for an excuse to cut loose on 'em. In fact, being hobbled with their hands tied behind them sure made escape improbable, to say the least. So when that sky started showing the light of false dawn, we weren't surprised to find them all present and accounted for. Just a mite surly, and stiff from lying hog-tied in the dirt, but not a man missing when we checked them out.

The first thing to do, of course, was to bury their dead. I'd been pretty close in my estimate of twenty when I first saw them charging in. Actually, there'd been eighteen; four were killed in the ambuscade and eight wounded, while somehow five escaped any injury at all. The eighteenth man fell from his horse and had been dragged to death.

At first light we found that one of the wounded had died during the night. He'd been badly hit, with a bullet in his thigh and another high up in the chest. We'd done all that we could, and I'd been half sure he was going to make it.

Altogether now there were seven dead, counting that man shot by the bearded feller. Two of the vaqueros had located the runaway horse, with what looked like a bloody bundle lying nearby. A poncho found behind the saddle served to wrap the body, and they'd brought it into the camp.

Vargas supervised while the four unwounded invaders dug the graves. I was some surprised when the bearded man, who we now knew as Lucius M. Dills, asked permission to say some words over the bodies. I was even more surprised when them killers hobbled over, shook off their hats, and stood by the open graves, heads bowed and eyes cast down.

It was an eerie scene. In the half-light of dawn Dills stood there with his hands bound behind his back and looked along the line of outlaws. "Men," he intoned, "here we see your comrades, who have given their lives in order that you may live. Remember this day! Remember how these aliens murdered your fellow troopers, and swear that you will never rest until we have our revenge! Until we have killed every one of these dirty foreigners or driven them from this land of ours. This land that is our rightful heritage! Amen!"

Wellsir! To say that I was surprised would sure be putting it mildly. Dumbfounded would be closer to the truth. I glanced over at Vargas, and he was shaking his head as if in disbelief.

"How can he say words like that?" he asked. "Is he loco, to say that we *murdered* these cowardly killers? They killed my vaqueros! They shot them down with no warning, like one would slaughter sheep, and mutilated their poor bodies. Can it be that this maniac actually *believes* what he is saying? Do these men feel that *we* are the aggressors?''

I put my arm over his shoulders. ''Don't you pay him no mind, Miguel. That man's nuttier than a peach orchard boar. He's jest plain crazy, and them men are jest as crazy as he is, believe me. Don Carlos will handle this, and thet bunch will pay for what they've done.''

A mumbled chorus of amens was interrupted by a bellow that came from over by the cook fire. *''Vengan! La comida está listo!''* Meaning, of course, that our food was ready. I tugged at Miguel's sleeve. ''C'mon, amigo. Let's go and git somethin' to eat before the cook throws it out.''

Santos, the one-legged cook, had coffee ready, and a kettle of beans, with chunks of beef, onions, and chiles bubbled over the open fire. Stacks of steaming hot tortillas off to one side and a crock of fiery salsa were there to add that special savor to a Mexican breakfast.

The prisoners' hobbles were loose enough that they could move slowly in a sort of shuffle, so we untied their hands, and they were led out in back in batches of four and given time to perform their morning routine. Afterwards they sat back down and were allowed to eat their fill. Then we tied their hands again and each one was given a cigarette.

Soon's everyone had eaten, the horses were saddled. Each prisoner had his hobbles untied before mounting. Once that was accomplished, his feet were tied together with a hobble that ran under the horse's belly and his hands lashed tight to the saddle horn. Halters were used on their horses, without reins, and the lead ropes on each were tied to the tails of the horses in front. There was plenty of grumbling when this was done, and several complained that we were endangering their lives.

''If my hoss steps in a hole,'' one said, ''I'm a dead man. Ain't no way I can keep from gittin' smashed like a stepped-on bug. It's un-human, I tell you!''

The vaquero who was doing the hobbling looked up at the grumbler. ''Don' ju worry, keeler! We gonna be choor to save ju for the riata! *Gaaahhh!*'' He made the gesture of a man strangling at the end of a rope.

Shortly after four o'clock we said our good-byes to those five who worked the cow camp. Vargas gave some last-minute instructions, telling Paco and Fernandez to continue working with the unbroke horses. ''Marindo,'' he said, ''I want you and Flaco to ride over to the camp at Indian's Draw and see what has happened there. I'm afraid you will find that they are all dead, but we must know for certain.

''If you find this to be true, then bury them, and be sure to mark their graves well. It may be that our *patrón* shall want them brought to the *estancia* and laid to rest with all of the others who have died for Rancho Montoncillo. Search for guns and leather gear and bring all you find back here, where it can be guarded. When you have done all this, choose one among you to ride to the rancho and make your report to Don Carlos. Keep your eyes open, because there could easily be more of these killers riding our range.''

The boys had nodded soberly and promised to be on their guard. Luis Marindo made a motion to me, and I bent down to hear what he had to say.

''Thees man weeth the *barba,* the hair on hees face, hees no' to be trusted, amigo. Ju keep jur eye on heem. I see heem ac' lak hees berry seek, bu' hees lak *vibora*—wha' ju call rattlesnake. When ju theenk hee's *muerto,* hee's cut ju weeth knife, or choot ju weeth gon. Ju unnerstan'?''

''Don't you worry your curly head, amigo. I figgered thet hombre for a snake first time I laid eyes on him. We'll be okay, Luis, and I'll be lookin' forward to seein' you soon.''

So we'd ridden out, with Vargas and me on the point, and eight of our nine remaining vaqueros riding swing and drag. A grim-faced rider led the column, with the body of the dead youngster, Nerio Lucero, wrapped in his serape on the leading packhorse, while the outlaws tagged on behind. It looked to be a grand day, with the sky clear and just enough of a breeze to be pleasant. Old Buck was fidgety and couldn't figger why we were moving so slow. He'd gotten a right good bait of corn and some sweet hay the boys had cut and stored in the barn and was all set for some real exercise.

After an hour or so we climbed down and walked for some time, just to have something different to do. If I had been the one to set the pace, I'd've had us at a lope, but I reckoned it would have been pure hell on them outlaws. Not that I worried about them suffering. They'd brought all this right smack down on themselves.

"You reckon Don Carlos *will* hang these fellers?" I asked. "Far as I'm concerned, he has full right to do so. It's got me some puzzled, Miguel. I mean, what thet feller Dills said over the graves. If I was a stranger and come amblin' by whilst he was sayin' them things, I'd of figgered he was in the right and you fellers was the outlaws. He sounded a lot like some of them circuit riders who traveled the hills of Kentucky. A touch more fire and brimstone and he'd have all the folks rollin' on the ground and hollerin' out loud. You reckon he *is* crazy, *compadre,* or was thet some kind of a trick he was playin' on his men?"

Miguel had dropped the bit out of his horse's mouth for a moment and was dabbing at it with a wet neckerchief. The bay was plumb enjoying it, and that was easy to see. Vargas waited until he had the bit back in place before he replied.

"There are many forms of lunacy, amigo. Some harm no one but themselves, while others are like beasts, and kill with no reason. When I was a student we read of the French Revolution and Napoleon Bonaparte. He *was* crazy! There isn't any doubt of that. But he believed he had a 'divine right' on his side, and he was convinced that what he did was proper for his people. I believe that is Dills's lunacy.

"His clothing seems to be parts of a uniform. Not just a private, but some kind of officer. Perhaps he suffered some terrible accident during the war. What doctors call mental breakdown. We'll probably never know. But one thing for sure—he believed every word he was saying, and he is the more dangerous for that very reason!"

Wellsir! I sure had no answer to that. I figgered something like what Miguel had said, but hadn't the right words to say it.

Vargas had to be right, because there wasn't any other logical explanation. We *knew* who'd started this here ruckus, and it sure hadn't been any of us.

It was coming on to noon when we sighted the ranch headquarters, and I for one was darn glad to see it. It'd been a long, tiresome ride, poking along like we had, and we were all pretty fed up with the threats and curses of Dills's men.

I was sorta surprised when none of the vaqueros that had been left behind came rushing out to greet us, but I remembered then that it was almost siesta time.

Vargas drew up and was looking ahead, his brow wrinkled and a puzzled expression on his face. He held up one arm in a signal to stop and turned to face me.

"Something is wrong, little brother," he said. "I do not see sentries waving from the towers, and no one has rung the bells. This is always done when a group of men approaches, and it is by a direct order from Don Carlos."

I taken a squint over that way, and I could see that what he said was true. There were men in them towers, but nobody was making any moves or signals.

"Well, what do you figger to do about it?" I asked. "We sure can't stay out here and wait. The horses are tired as heck, and so are the men. What do you say? Shall you and I ride on ahead and find out what's goin' on? Leave the rest here until we find out if everything's all right?"

He nodded, but he sure looked plenty worried. A crook of his finger brought up one of the vaqueros riding swing, so's he could give the man instructions. The rider taken off his hat and listened respectfully, then backed off and walked his horse back to the others.

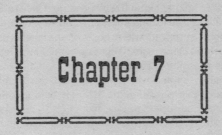

Chapter 7

When we'd loped in closer to the ranch buildings, we both saw that the sentries in the towers were wearing blue uniform coats, and most were bearded. They made no moves to fire on us, but merely looked down curious-like as we rode up.

"What's this all about?" I said, low-voiced. "What would the Army be doin' here, Miguel? Reckon they've tangled with some of Dills's bandits and are here to tell us about it?"

Vargas shook his head and glanced over at me. "I have no idea, amigo, but we'll soon find out."

As we trotted around a corner of the wall and approached the corral gate, I could see a group of strange men leaning indolently against the rails, all heavily armed and all in blue Yankee uniforms. One with yellow chevrons on both of his sleeves hailed us pleasantly as we rode in.

"Afternoon, gents! What can I do for you today? That a pack train you men have out yonder? You lookin' to water or feed your stock? We got plenty, and we're willing to share. Just step down, and I'll treat you to some fine whiskey."

Miguel was trembling with rage. "Who are you *cabrones*, and what are you doing here? Where is Don Carlos? What the hell is going on here?" He reached down for the Winchester under his knee.

"Just you hold it right there!" The sergeant's manners and his expression changed. There were audible clicks as a dozen rifles were cocked and suddenly pointing at us.

"Don't try it, Miguel," I hollered desperately. "They'd shoot us both before you could git it out."

"You're a smart young feller," the sergeant told me. "I reckon you go to the head of the class. Now just you climb down off of them horses, and keep your hands in plain sight. I don't know who you are, but I can tell you this. Try to draw a weapon and you're dead meat. Lively, now! Get down here and grab a handful of them clouds."

Old Miguel's face was almost purple, he was so mad, but I saw no reason for us to die until we found out what was going on. Once on the ground, two of the soldiers came toward us and taken our belt guns. I was hoping they'd pass up my shoulder rig, but they'd obviously done this many times and knew where to look.

"This ain't no ordinary cowhand," he said as he held the gun up for the sergeant to see. "Maybe he's one of them big *pistoleros* we been hearin' so much about—a paid gunhand working for one of the ranchers here in the valley."

"Nah," the sergeant scoffed with a grin. "That's not no *pistolero*. He's a white man, and them gunmen are *Messicans*. This is Comanche country, and ever'body carries more'n one.

"Besides," he went on, "big as he is, he's just a youngster. A smart one, who knows when the odds are against him, and don't try no smart tricks." He stared up at me. "How tall are you, kid? Must be close on to seven foot."

"I got a question of my own," I said to him. "What're you men doin' around here? This here's private property, owned by a responsible citizen, and you got no reason to be on it. What have you done with the owner, Don Carlos Montoncillo, a good friend of mine?" As I asked the questions, I had me an idea I wasn't gonna like the answers.

The sergeant taken another look at me and apparently was not too happy with what he saw. Mebbe he figgered that we were some kind of lawmen or something, because he thought a moment before he gave me an answer.

"Your precious Don Carlos is under arrest," he said. "We have confisticated this here land, 'cause he's about to stand trial as a traitor. Him 'n' his kind plan to take over a big part of Texas, and we're here to stop him. Only us American folks got a right to live here. Not these here furriners."

I had a sort of empty feeling in my belly. I'd been on track when I'd figgered mebbe these men were part of Dills's bunch; I was sure of that now. What to do? How could me 'n' Vargas warn them others, the vaqueros who were holding Dills and his men as prisoners? Without them as hostages we had nothing left to bargain with and would have to give in.

"That's not a pack train out there," I told him. "Might be closer to the truth if you called it an army. Not a big one, but every man is heavily armed and a dead shot. You'd best think about it before doin' any shootin', because that might jest git you killed. Now take us to Don Carlos, and do it right away!"

It was plain to see that he was none too happy about the situation. Undoubtedly they had depended on the bunch of killers led by Dills to eliminate any opposition. He studied for a moment, then made his decision.

"Tie them horses up," he told one of the men. "You 'n' the Mex can come with me." He pointed toward the main building. A pair of uniform-clad men fell in behind us with guns held at the ready, and we started walking. The sergeant kept his hand on his holstered revolver as he went on ahead. We saw no sign of Sanchez or any of the servants, and I feared the lot of them might have been butchered.

I was prepared for the worst as we entered the dim gloom of the main hall, but it was even more than I had imagined. Carlos was lying on a pallet, blood staining the shoulder of his jacket, and Esperanza was kneeling by his side. A basin of hot water held surgical instruments, and she was about to remove the jacket. She looked up as we entered and gasped in surprise and disappointment. From the dark rings around her eyes, I could tell she'd been crying, but right now her lips were set in a thin line, and her face was a cold mask of an inner fury that could boil over at any minute. She didn't say a word, nor did I.

Sitting in Carlos's thronelike chair was a sorta stout, middle-aged man dressed in a gray suit with wide lapels, a heavy gold watch chain looped across his middle. He looked us over, his small mouth pursed in what seemed displeasure.

"Well," he snapped as the sergeant made a gesture toward us. "Who are these men, and why have you brought them before me? Can't you take care of these little matters all by yourself? Must I lead you around by the hand?"

A thin, cadaverous man was standing by his side, a naked, gleaming saber in one hand. His uniform was that of a Union officer, and captain's bars were on his shoulder boards. He stepped slightly to one side, and behind him I could see the crumpled body of little Poco Luce, lying with arms outflung and cocked eye staring sightlessly at the ceiling. He was stone dead.

Suddenly something snapped inside my head, and I rushed blindly forward, hands reaching for the throat of the seated man. With one tremendous effort I lifted him bodily out of the chair and held him above my head, where his arms and legs waved madly, like a beetle on a pin. With one grasp on his throat and the other around a leg, I swung him back for an instant, then threw him half the length of the room. Out of the corner of one eye I could see the sergeant trying to tug his pistol from the holster, and I smacked him alongside the head with the flat of one big hand, knocking him down sprawling on the floor.

A rifle went off in my ear, and I felt the heat of muzzle blast, but not enough to burn. Reaching back, I grabbed the empty rifle with both hands, jerking the man toward me and smashing the top of my head into his face. I felt the bones in his nose crumple, and blood poured down over his chin as he slumped to the floor, out cold.

Esperanza screamed, and I started to turn. The captain had his saber raised high in the air and had already started a downward slash. His teeth were bared in a grimace, and cords stood out on his neck from the strain.

I threw up my left arm as I leaped toward him and felt the blade glance on the bone, then bite deeply into the left side of my head. A terrible, searing pain lanced through my cheek, and I could feel myself falling. A kick thudded against my ribs, and there was more pain. I tried to get up, but there was no strength in my arms. Somewhere, off in the distance, I heard more screams. Then blackness rushed in. . . .

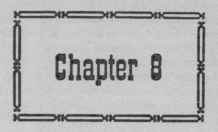

Chapter 8

The old man stirred fitfully. His eyelids fluttered, blinked open, the incredibly blue orbs contrasting vividly with the dark leathery texture of his deeply lined face. He groaned. Damn an old man's bladder, he thought to himself. Only a moment before, he'd been dreaming of a sun-washed meadow in which a husky youngster, his mirror image, chased down mares and colts and counted his natural increase.

Throwing back the blanket, he swung his feet to the plank floor and groaned again, his hand in the small of his back. There must be a way to grow old less painfully! All of them bones he'd broken and muscles he'd pulled as a lad, he sure was paying for now! Reaching out, he snared his pants off a chair back and pulled them on. Boots came next, and he hobbled out the door and headed for the corral in back.

Must be about four o'clock, he thought to himself. Faint light in the skies to the east meant dawn was maybe an hour or so away. Today was Sunday, and Abigail would insist the service be held, with him reading the Bible. Julia was real big with child, and with any kind of luck he might soon see his first great-grandchild. A boy he could train, as his pa had trained him. A boy who would grow up knowing horses and horse ways, and loving them, as he had done. A boy who'd be trusting of the Lord, as he had always been.

Closing the privy door, he started for the gate. Something caught his eye, and he stared intently, his eyes wide open. There was something on the hillside a quarter of a mile away that shouldn't be there. A dark mass that moved slowly down the hill as he stood there watching.

His breath caught for a moment, then he was running, his bowed, rheumatic legs carrying him toward the front, and the room of his son-in-law. "Milo!" he yelled. "Milo! Come and see! Wake up, Milo! We got us some trouble!"

By this time he was through the bunkhouse door and fumbling for a match. Scratching it alight across the seat of his pants, he cursed as the stick broke and the flame burned his fingers.

A door came open in the partition dividing the room, and a tall, ghostly figure in white underwear asked him sleepily, "What's goin' on, Eli? What're you doin' hollerin' this time of night? You ain't had 'nother one of them nightmares again, have you? It's turrible, wakin' a man from his sound sleep like this. 'Specially when he was up with a sickly orphan calf the night before."

The old man had another match in his hand. "Look out the winder," he hissed. "Over there, towards the hillside. I'm 'fraid we got us some comp'ny, Milo, and they ain't makin' a Sunday social call." He started to scratch the match.

Milo McCowan was still half asleep, but that didn't mean he was any less cautious. Reaching out, he grabbed the oldster's arm with a hamlike hand.

"Let's leave off lightin' thet lamp just yet. No reason to let them know we're awake, Eliakim. I see what you mean. Nighttime callers are either Injuns or somebody else up to no good. You go 'n' wake Ma 'n' Julia, then—"

"What's goin' on, Milo? What're you 'n' Grandpa doin'? It ain't even daylight yet." Another underwear-clad figure, a hand on Milo's arm, whispered hoarsely, his eyes wide with curiosity and wonderment.

"We ain't sure yet, Sam. We got some visitors comin' over yonder, and I doubt they're friendly. You'd best git the womenfolk up and warn them not to show a light." He looked down at the slender teenaged boy. "Best git on britches, though, before you do anythin' else."

"Yessir, Milo! I'm on my way!" In his eagerness, he ran into a chair and sent it crashing to the floor. "Durn!" he muttered. "Ain't nothin' never in its rightful place!"

Milo looked over at the old man. "We got us a few more minutes," he said. "I best get on some clothes my own self. I reckon you'll want to use thet old Spencer carbine, so git it out, and fill your pockets with cartridges. I'll be gone no more'n a minute. Wait. . . ." He caught hold of Eli's arm.

"I jest remembered. I filled up some tubes with shells for the Spencer, and they're in thet Blakeslee loader case."

The old man nodded and groped his way across the room, a hand out in front of him to ward off obstructions. When his hand came in contact with the rifle rack, he felt his way to the far end, where his favorite weapon was standing. A case filled with the loading tubes went over one shoulder, and he flipped the gate in the carbine's butt over to one side, one tube of seven filling the magazine tube. Jacking the action open, he held down the protruding cartridge and fed another into the chamber. Closing the action and setting the heavy hammer at half cock readied him for whatever might come.

Milo came in, tucking his shirttails into his pants. The sky had lightened considerably, and visibility was becoming much better. Taking a quick look out the window, he saw that the group of horsemen were now within three hundred yards, slowly moving at no more than a walk.

"Close all them shutters," he rasped at the old man. "We got to let them fellers know they're treadin' on dangerous and deadly ground, comin' in here 'thout no invite."

Turning to the rifle rack, he selected two full-stocked and set-triggered Sharps rifles. Although they were percussion-cap fired, they could be loaded through the breech with linen cartridges. Each one contained the proper charge and included a large conical bullet weighing 475 grains. With the action levered open the breechblock dropped, and a cartridge could be inserted in the chamber. Closing the action caused a knifelike edge on the block to shear off a portion of the cartridge and allow the powder to be exposed.

First off, Milo exploded a cap on each of the rifles and made sure the nipples were open, then loaded both guns. Then he moved over to a shuttered window with one in each hand.

The incoming riders were now no more than two hundred yards away, and it was time to change their minds. Thrusting the long-barreled rifle through a port, he took a fine sight on a big rock to the left of the leading horseman and touched off a round. Before the ensuing cloud of dirty white smoke rose and obscured the target, he saw the bullet hit, sending bits of rock in all directions and causing the terrified horses, stung by the fragments, to rear and buck.

Several riders were thrown, some horses bolted, and a few men were able to control their mounts. Shouts and curses of rage and anger could be plainly heard as the startled raiders milled in confusion. Milo's ears were ringing from the close-confined explosion, but he was jubilant.

"Will you lookee there, Eli!" he shouted. "Reckon they'd ruther talk, about now. Mebbe I'll jest give 'em another of them, so's they'll know we ain't foolin' around." Once more a thunderous roar echoed in the room, and, looking out, Milo could see that the whole bunch were in full retreat. One of the riders, who had been thrown from his horse, was holding desperately to another man's stirrup and running like his very life depended on it. All were panic-stricken and fleeing for their lives from the hidden marksman.

Milo ran a brush down both bores to clean out the fouled rifling and carefully reloaded. Above the stink of burned black powder he could smell the fragrance of coffee. The women must be up, he thought to himself, and breakfast would soon be ready. Though it was still early, he felt the pangs of hunger and could hardly wait for them to call.

"What's thet out there?" Eli asked. "Look's like a white flag thet one of them fellers is wavin'. Could be they're wantin' to dicker some. You know, Milo," he went on, "them fellers looked to be wearin' blue jackets. You don't s'pose they could be sojers, do you? What would sojers be doing on this ranch at this ungodly hour? Don't s'pose that feller Lieutenant O'Dowd might be with this bunch?"

Milo shook his head. "O'Dowd wouldn't be sneakin' that way. He'd've left his bunch behind a ways and come in here by hisself. 'Sides, he'd have waited until the sun was up."

While still fifty yards from the ranch house, the man who was carrying the white flag dismounted and walked alongside his horse, careful to keep the horse's body between him and the concealed rifleman.

"Thet's far enough," Milo called out. "Who are you, what is your business here, and what do you want from me?"

"This here is Deputy U.S. Marshal Len Chidden, and I have a federal warrant for your arrest. That is, if you are Milo Mc-Cowan, and I figure you must be."

"What's the charge, Marshal Chidden? How could I do anythin' wrong when I'm here on the ranch mindin' my own business and havin' nothin' to do with snakes like you."

"You'd better watch that mouth, McCowan. This here is an official warrant, and I'm here to place you under arrest."

"You ain't answered my question, Chidden. What does it say on the warrant? What am I supposed to have done?"

"Don't you be smart with me, McCowan. You know full well what your crime has been. Inciting Indians, who are legally wards of the government, to riot and mayhem. Wasn't for the murderous ex-Rebs like you, this state of Texas would be an easy place to live. Folks wouldn't have to worry about them Indians murdering them in their beds."

"What Injuns am I supposed to have 'incited,' Chidden? I

don't have much truck with Injuns. You oughta know thet. We got us some dead ones buried up there on the knoll, and they weren't exactly friends of ours. I think mebbe you and the rest of thet bunch better head on out of here before I lose my patience. You hear me? Git! If I see you pokin' around here again, I'm not goin' to deliberately miss. *Comprendes*, Marshal Len Chidden?''

Hastily the marshal hoisted his bulk into the saddle. A clumsiness born of fear caused him to miss his first step, and he fell heavily as the horse shied away. Furious, the plump lawman grabbed at his horse, causing the animal to shy even more. Virtually beside himself with rage, he threw the white flag to the ground, and that did it. Terrified, the horse bolted, leaving the unhappy man behind.

Turning, he'd taken but a few steps when Milo called out, ''I'm givin' you thirty seconds to git outta range, mister marshal. You'd best git to movin', unless you want a bullet in that big behind of yours.''

''No!'' the marshal shrieked. ''Don't shoot, McCowan! This ain't no way to treat a federal officer, you know. I'm only doing my duty, and you're making it worse on yourself.'' The man was almost paralyzed with fright, but this didn't affect his running. Awkwardly, he headed out across the prairie, with a running waddle that set everyone in the McCowan house laughing until the tears ran down their cheeks.

''Uh uh uh, *hooee!* Did you see thet fat old devil movin' out?'' Milo was paralyzed with mirth. The boy, Sam, taken to imitating the marshal's waddle and sent Milo off into a hysterical outburst of hearty laughter.

Chidden was still in easy range when the others began to fire on the house. There was no way the bullets could penetrate the double-block adobe walls, but it was a nuisance.

A call from the kitchen caused Milo to lean the rifles against the wall. Breakfast was ready, and he still hadn't had a chance to wash up. Turning to Sam and old Eli, he grinned. ''I don't reckon we have to worry about them fellers chargin' in here. Leastways, not for a while. I'm gonna go out back to the washhouse and make myself presentable. You two are welcome to come along if you're of a mind.''

"I've already been," retorted the old man. "Right now I sure could use a cup of your mama's coffee, and that's where I'm headed. I'll tell her you'll be along d'rectly.''

"Come along, Sam.'' Milo reached out and ruffled a hand through the boy's curly hair. "Well, young'un, how do you feel about becomin' a McCowan? Are you happy here with us? Everybody treatin' you all right?''

The boy looked up at him with naked love in his eyes. "I reckon I feel like I've died and gone to heaven, Milo. You and your maw have made me feel like I'm one of the family. A body couldn't ask for much more'n thet. I sure do wish Rush would come home, though. I miss him somethin' fierce.''

"So do I, Sam. So do I.'' Milo's eyes misted over, and for a moment he was afraid the tears might come. He sorely missed his older brother, his companion of almost five long years of war. He knew it was because of his marriage to Julia that Rush had stayed up north. It wasn't my fault alone, he said to himself. Falling in love isn't what a man plans. It just happens, and there ain't no way to prevent it once the bug has bitten you. He'd had no idea that Rush was even interested in Julia. Matter of fact, Rush hadn't showed any particular like for the woman. He had even tried to run Julia and her grandfather off when he'd found their wagon and horse herd on CMC land.

Well, what's done is done, and there ain't no way for a man in love to step aside, especially when the girl had told him of her feelings. He looked down at the boy beside him, who was manfully trying to match his stride, and he recalled that day in the *brasada* when the boy's woebegone horse poked his head through the brush and they'd heard the story of the boy's orphaning. Pridefully the boy had given them his name, Samuel Walker Wyeth, after a famous Texas Ranger, hero of the Mexican War, and personal friend of Samuel Colt.

They had watched him wolf down the remnants of their noon meal after first staking his horse on good green grass. A "dogie"—a stray, orphan calf—he'd wiggled like a puppy as Maw taken him in her arms and told him he'd found a home.

Once in the washhouse, Milo watched as Sam scrubbed his face and hands, dunked his head, and meticulously combed his hair, careful to make a part, as Maw had taught him. Glancing up, Sam grinned. "How's thet, Milo? Do I look okay?"

Milo nodded, his face full of lather and his razor poised on his cheek. "Good enough to go to a funeral," he told him. "You're gonna have to forgit some of your chores today," he went on. "With them fellers out there waitin', the horse herd'll have to stay in the corral. Say! Thet liver bay of Rush's, the one he calls Pard, he could stand some exercise. Lightly brought him over from their place the other day. I reckon you already know thet, huh? Well, you might ride him around the corral a spell, then give him a good rubdown so he won't feel neglected. Last thing Rush told Lightly, back in Abilene, was to make sure the horse didn't git fat. Now you be careful, you hear? Stay close in to the walls, 'cause you never know when one of them hombres might try a shot or two with a long-range rifle."

Quickly he finished shaving and wiped his face. "Let's git our rears into Maw's kitchen and see what she's servin' for breakfast. All thet excitement's got my belly rumblin', and I'm ready to really shovel it in."

"Me too," the boy replied. Then: "Say, Milo! You must have kilt lots of fellers back durin' the war. Didn't it bother you none when all thet was goin' on? Wasn't it hard for you to shoot right at a feller, with him a-lookin' right square at you, and bein' a white man 'n' all? 'Nother thing. Wasn't you ever skeered, with them big cannons firin', balls skippin' along, and sometimes flyin' over your head? Didn't you jest once wish you was back home, and wish there never was a war at all?"

Milo put a hand on Sam's shoulder and turned him around. "Son," he said, "there was very few times when me 'n' brother Rush wasn't scared, but there was never a time when both of us weren't wishin' thet war hadn't started. When brother is fightin' brother, as happened many times back then, nothin' can justify a war like thet. But I learned one thing. The best defense is a good offense. You can't back down.

"It's jest like them fellers out there. Thet marshal is playin' somebody's game. He knows we ain't incitin' none of the Injuns, but he's bound to arrest me no matter what. If I was to back down, to jest give up peaceable and allow him to cart me off to jail, then first thing you know Maw would be next, or Eli, or mebbe even you 'n' Julia. We'd never ever see this ranch ever again. Probably be lucky if they didn't jest kill us out of hand.

"No, war ain't nice, nor is killin' another man, but you will find out that some men are greedy. Give 'em a finger and they'll want your whole hand. We built up this here old ranch with our hopes and our sweat 'n' hard work, and no one is gonna take it away from us. If it means killin', then we will do what has to be done. Them men may have us penned in here, but we got enough eats to last us for a month, and we got plenty of powder and ball. Mainly, we got the pride and determination to hold on to what's ours, and that means the right is on our side. It'll turn out, so don't you worry."

Little was said over breakfast. Maw McCowan had cooked a big meal, and everyone did justice to what she'd prepared. Like old Eli said, it might be quite a while before meals and such could be taken together. Some of them would have to be on guard while the others did more mundane things.

Julia, her belly swollen with the child she was carrying, was as cheerful as the rest. She might have to rely on Maw when her time came, if they were still under siege. She had hoped the surgeon from Fort Davis, Dr. Weisel, would be able to attend, but under the present conditions that seemed unlikely. No rider would be able to get out, nor would any of them want to leave, with the family threatened.

Pushing back from the table, Milo rolled a cigarette, and Eli lighted his pipe. "You reckamember when Lysander brung you in on his horse after you'd been shot up by them Shaler fellers?" Eli asked. "Wellsir, Rush made hisself up a sorta warning alarm, usin' some wire and a lot of empty airtights tied on about ten foot apart. Him and me strung thet wire about fifty feet out from the walls. Jest laid it along the ground. It worked jest fine, 'cep'n you 'n' Lysander was about kilt when his horse got tangled up and turned a cart-wheel. Might not be a bad idee, us doin' the same thing. We'd have to wait until after dark tonight so's them sojers couldn't see us layin' it out.''

"Good idea," Milo told him. "Why don't you 'n' Sam build it up, and we'll string it out tonight. 'Nother thing. We'd best all wear a gun from now on, and thet'll include Julia. I ain't sure how you're gonna git a gunbelt around thet big belly, honey, but we'll find a way.''

"I'm gonna go right now and lay out the long guns. The chances are they'll try to sneak in tonight, and the horse corral might seem the easiest to breech. So I'll load some shotguns and put them in the shed out back. I've got some combustible paper, and I'll use thet to make up some spares, so them scatterguns will reload fast. Main thing to remember is not to try taking prisoners. If one of them gits in this close, don't ask him to put up his hands. Jest go ahead and shoot. Aim for his body, 'cause thet's the easiest piece of him to hit and the surest way to make a killin' shot.''

"I cain't he'p wishin' thet Rush were here.'' Abigail Mc-Cowan looked earnestly at her son. "It ain't thet I ain't got jest as much confidence in you, Milo, but Rush allus has things worked out. He picks him a plan, and he goes on out and gits it done. Ain't nobody in God's world c'n stop him when his mind's made up. He'd charge the fires of hell, and him with no more'n a bucket of water, and Satan hisself he would run for kiver. Thet boy's got him a charm on him, and he'll allus git most anythin' he wants.'' Her face clouded with worry. "I sure do hope he's doin' all right now.''

"I understand, Maw, but don't you worry thet pretty head of yours. We'll make out jest fine. Heck! There can't be more'n twenty of them fellers out there, and thet ain't but four apiece for us McCowans.''

Julia put her hand on his arm. "Be careful, Milo. You have a son not too far off, and he'll need his father. I'm in good shape, and we can hold out here for a long time. We don't none of us have to take any foolish chances.''

"Who said anythin' about takin' chances? Why, this here is

more like a turkey shoot. We're in here behind them old 'dobe walls, safe as a babe in his mother's arms. We'll be jest fine, honey, and I got me a notion thet help might jest be along before you know it.''

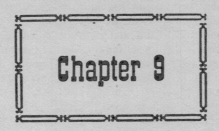

Chapter 9

Why is it so dark, and why am I so cold? Can't a feller get him a blanket when he's freezing half to death? But it ain't cold. Not now. I'm burning up. Where am I? Water would sure taste good about now, but there ain't none. The water's just for them as really needs it. But I'm thirsty as hell. I earned that water. Where is everybody? Why did they take away the water? There ain't nobody can help. I'm all alone, and I'm hurting. Hurting bad.

Sorry, Paw, I can't help it. I ain't *trying* to cry. The tears come natural, 'cause of this awful pain. Why don't you try to understand? I done my best, but he whupped me sump'n fierce. Sure, I remember. I remember now.

I'd come home crying that day, ashamed of my tears, head streaming blood from the bully's club. Paw tried to comfort me, saying: "Even a man will cry, Lysander, but a man'll dry his tears, though he can still feel the pain, and he'll call on something deep down inside him to git his revenge. Now you listen to your old paw, and you remember good! None of us Choctaw folks ever gits mad; we jest gits even."

But Paw, I'd cried, I hurt, and it's this pain that's making me cry. The pain . . . My head throbbed, and behind my eyes a burning, searing fire rose, and I felt the hot welling of unshed tears. I tried to lift one hand to my head, but my arm wouldn't, or couldn't, move.

I was shaking with the cold, but I could feel sweat running down my back and beading my face. I cried out and felt a cool hand on my cheek, heard a sweet voice whispering soft endearments and calling my name.

"Lysander, dearest. *Ay, mi corazón. Mi amor de todo de mi corazón!* It is I, your Esperanza. I am here, darling Lysander, close by your side and aching to help you. Open your eyes, my love. Please open your eyes!"

A damp cloth passed across my face, and I tried. Then, with an effort, I forced my eyes open and saw Esperanza's beautiful face close to mine. She smiled, though her eyes were brimming with tears. Then that blackness came back, and I was falling, turning and twisting, the sickness pulling at my guts, and a bitterness in my mouth.

I awakened with the warm sun in my face and its brightness hurting my eyes. I blinked and looked up at the ceiling . . . and I remembered. Half fearful, I glanced down at my left arm and found it heavily bandaged but still there. My head was aching, and, reaching up gingerly with my right hand, I felt a bandage covering the left side of my head and wrapped around my forehead. It was painful to the touch.

Esperanza was there, but she was sound asleep in a chair, her head down and her long black hair falling to her knees. On a small table between us was a jug of water and some glasses, and suddenly I was very thirsty. Reaching out with my good hand, I tried to lift that jug, and there wasn't any strength in my arm. It came down hard, and the glasses made a tinkling clatter, waking Esperanza.

"Oh, Lyse! You're awake! Oh, darling, I've been so very worried! You've been so sick, and the fever . . ." She leaned over me and pressed her lips to mine, then showered kisses on my cheeks, my forehead, and again on my lips.

"How long have I been here, honey, and jest exactly where are we now? How's Carlos, and Vargas? Where *is* Vargas?"

"We are here in my room at the rancho, and you have been unconscious for more than a week. Father's fine, but hasn't spoken to anyone, not even me. He grieves for Poco Luce as a man would grieve for an only son, and he blames himself. Perhaps he feels that if he hadn't trained Poco Luce as his bodyguard the boy wouldn't have fought to the death. There were eleven bullet wounds in his body when he finally fell to the floor. He was still trying to cock his rifle as his last breath was taken. He was very brave, and he cared very much for my father." The tears came again, and she bent in her grief.

"Pobrecito hermanito! He was not handsome, but misshapen as he appeared, his heart was good. His mother is grieving, but she is very proud of what he did. She is our *cocinera,* our cook here in the house. She has tried to get my father to eat regular meals, but he takes only enough to keep alive and well. He stays in his bed and will not even sit up."

"How about Miguel Vargas? Where is he? Did he git hurt like me? Is he all right?"

"Miguel Vargas and the others are locked up in the bunkhouses, except for a few servants who are being put to use. The *yanquis* have taken over the main house, or most of it."

"What about the vaqueros, and the prisoners we taken? We had one of the leaders, some feller named Dills. Did any of our boys git away, or did they try to attack the house?"

"They weren't given a chance, Lyse. The soldiers said we would all be killed unless they came in and surrendered to these pigs. The eight vaqueros rode in and gave up all the prisoners and their guns. They too are locked up."

"What'd you say? Eight vaqueros came in? But honey, we

had nine boys with us, and the body of one who'd got killed last night—I mean the last night before we came here to the ranch. One of 'em must have snuck away. Mebbe we ain't so bad off after all. Leastways we got somebody that can tell Milo and the rest what's happened. Don't you fret your pretty head, honey. Milo'll git us outta here, and it won't be long before we're free of this trash.''

"I don't think so, Lyse. I overheard two of the soldiers talking yesterday, and they said your ranch is under siege. It's surrounded, and they expected to take it soon.''

My heart skipped a beat. How many of these fellers did they have? Must be a regular army. I looked up at my sweet Esperanza, and her face was so sad and discouraged.

"Don't worry, honey,'' I told her. "Milo will find a way. Thet house of ours is like a fort, and it'll take more'n an army to break inside. Him and Maw, they'll figger a way to beat this bunch. Meantimes we'd best git to thinkin' some our own selves.'' A thought struck me.

"Where are my chaps, honey? My *chaparejos,* you know? If they're here in the room, fetch 'em over here, will you? We might jest use what's in one of the pockets. That is, if it wasn't found by one of them soldiers.''

She brought me the chaps, and that Moore derringer was in the pocket, along with the three extra cartridges. I turned the barrel to one side and made sure it was still loaded up, then stuck it down alongside my leg. In doing that, the feel of bare skin made me realize that I was naked as a jaybird. I didn't even have on any underwear.

"Say, who was it taken off all my clothes?'' I asked. "I ain't got on a stitch. Was it Vargas? Did he help you take care of me? Was it him thet stripped me naked?''

"Miguel helped carry you up the stairs, but then the men took him away and locked him in with the others.''

"Well? You ain't answered my question. Who taken off my durned clothes, and where are my duds now?''

Her face was reddening, and she turned away. "You were unconscious, Lysander dear. Your clothing was soaked with blood from your wounds. It had to be washed, and that's all been taken care of. You can have them now if you wish. We *are* to be married, dearest. You know that, and surely you'd not mind my undressing you. It had to be done.''

She shrugged. ''That's really not all I have to confess to you, Lysander. The first two days and nights your fever was so bad, and you were shaking with chills. I knew you must get some rest or your wounds would never heal. I held you in my arms and let the warmth of my bare body take the chills away. You went to sleep immediately.''

I was scandalized. I didn't know *what* to say. This well-bred woman had actually gotten in my bed naked and held me in her arms? Why, I never heard of such a thing! I'd never even *seen* a naked woman, much less had one hold on to me! We *were* planning to get married, sure, but weren't there limits to what a decent woman would do, no matter the reasons?

Then I realized what an ordeal it must have been. How a sensitive, convent-bred girl like Esperanza would've died before doing anything she thought was wrong. I was so proud of her. There was no doubt I owed her my life. Without her courage and skill I would certainly have died.

I reached out and taken her by the hand. ''Honey, I am sorry, honest. I shouldn't never've hollered at you like a mean old grizzly bear. Forgive me, sweetheart. I'm really touched by what you've done, and uncommon grateful. Believe me. I reckon I *would* have died, hadn't been for you.

''Tell me,'' I said, drawing her down to where she was on the bed sitting next to me. ''How bad is it? All I can remember is that blade comin' down on my arm, then hittin' me alongside my head. Did it cut pretty deep? Is my ear still there? I'd look pretty funny with only one ear.''

Her expression was a sober one. ''It cut very deep, but ahead of your ear. I'm afraid that you will have a very bad scar, Lyse. I tried my best to bring the ends as close as I could, but it required more than thirty stitches to close up the wound. I used sinew from a deer—some that our leather worker uses. He keeps a quantity on hand for close stitching on boots, and things like that. I washed it thoroughly in some of father's whiskey before sewing up the wound.''

"How about my arm?" I frowned and tried my best to raise it from the bed. It just flat wouldn't move. Worried me a lot, 'cause a one-armed cowboy ain't much use to nobody, and I didn't know much else, 'cep'n cattle.

Sensing how I felt, she was quick to reassure me. "There isn't any muscle damage," she told me. "If you'll look just a bit closer, you will find that I've tied that arm down so you wouldn't injure it any further." She smiled.

I sorta rolled a bit and saw what she meant. A pair of latigo whangs were around my forearm at wrist and elbow. I felt pretty foolish as I traced them down to a slat in the framing of the bed. "And here I was," I told her, "thinkin' this arm of mine was plumb paralyzed. I tried my hardest to reach up to my head, and jest couldn't even make this budge. I'll tell you the truth, honey. I was really scared. I was certain sure thet arm was ruint for the rest of my life."

We both laughed—my laughter born of relief, and hers from the pure pleasure of knowing I loved her, understood in full what she'd gone through, and was finally on the mend.

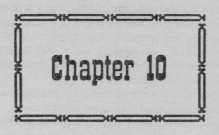

Chapter 10

The jail in the village of Ojinaga was nestled underneath the spreading limbs of an ancient jacaranda tree, and thick adobe walls insured its coolness even on the hottest day of the year. A border town in the state of Chihuahua, Ojinaga had hosted some of the most infamous of badmen, both Mexican and American, at various times in its history. Over the years, the population had alternately increased and declined as citizens of Presidio, the Texas town across the Rio Grande, fled from all-out attacks by the Apache Indians.

Right now it was an American who lolled on a cot in one corner of a high-ceilinged cell, and he seemed happy enough. Why shouldn't he be? he thought to himself. The food here was good, if your palate was tuned to highly seasoned meals, and there was plenty of it. No one seemed to mind when you spent most of your time dozing, and there was always someone who'd play checkers or dominoes if you were so inclined.

A tall, sparely built man, there wasn't much about him to make him stand out in a crowd unless you looked real close. It was his hands, and their size. Huge, knotted, and scarred across the knuckles, they hung on wrists that were thick and corded with muscle; they looked more like cedar fence posts than wrists, both in diameter and durability.

Idly he reached down behind the cot and picked up a bit of chalk. Studying the number of short lines marked on the wall beside him, he made a diagonal slash across a series of four. Twenty-five days he'd spent in this cell, and according to the mandate of the *alcalde* he now had only five more months and five days left to serve. A lot of time for no more than he had done.

He had explained his purpose to the *cantinero* upon first entering the Cantina Concho. Mainly he wanted to be all by himself so that he could do something about his thirst, one that had been building for weeks, as he broke horses for the wealthy Don Francisco de la Ochoa, on the Texas side of what he called Rio Bravo. Something in the perverse nature of the portly rancher had caused him to flaunt liquor in front of the *jinete gringo,* the American bronc buster. He did all this knowing the problem the rider had with alcohol, and he refused to allow anyone to offer the man a drink. It'd been no easy thing to stand unaffected as Ochoa had counted out the silver pesos and warned him of the effect alcohol could have on the human body. But he'd held back, knowing that an almost inexhaustible supply lay just across the river.

Tequila had been his first choice, taken straight, with a dash of salt and a bite of lemon. As was the custom in a Mexican cantina, each drink was served in a fresh glass, and the empties were left on the table so that the *cantinero* was able to keep a reckoning of the bill. Soon he'd been forced to take another table, as his own was covered with empty shot glasses, and some of the other patrons marveled at what they termed his *capacidad*, his tremendous capacity.

When the supply of shot glasses ran out, someone had suggested he try pulque, a milky liquor made from the fermented juice of the maguey plant. Served in earthen crocks, fresh from the shed out in back, this had gone down like milk from a cow, but its effects were disastrous.

After downing his third crock, he found it very difficult to stand, much less walk, and had called for his bill. Now, how he planned to leave he really didn't know, but he wanted to make sure the reckoning was paid before he tried.

Peering owlishly at the adjoining table, he made an attempt to count the glasses but came up with a different total each time. A friendly bystander offered to help while the bartender was proffering the bill, and somehow the argument had gotten started.

The *cantinero* had made the mistake of hitting him with an empty crock, and he'd thrown the unfortunate man through the front door, which was closed at the time. Some of the other patrons joined in the melee, and the fight was on. Many had never particularly liked the *cantinero*, feeling that he overcharged his customers from time to time, and they were glad to help destroy his cantina, enthusiastically smashing every table and chair in the place, and even getting in a punch or two at the owner and the few who had taken his side.

Somewhere along the line the local law had shown up, and they had helped finish the job. The next morning he'd been taken before the magistrate, still reeling from the effects, and his bankroll had passed into the hands of the *cantinero*. To insure that this would not be repeated, the *alcalde* added the six months in jail to his punishment.

Hearing a key grating in the lock, he swung his feet over to the floor and watched as a middle-aged Mexican entered. In his hand he held a sheaf of papers, and glancing down at them, he spoke.

"Your name is McCowan?" he asked.

"That's right," the American replied. "Trace McCowan, in

the flesh. Why? You got more charges you're gonna find on me? Hell, man, I paid the damages. What more d'ye want?''

"Do you mind if I sit down?'' the man asked. ''I have more questions, and it's been a long ride.''

The American grinned and moved to one end of the cot. ''I don't have much to offer,'' he replied, waving a hand toward the unoccupied end. ''But you're more'n welcome to share.''

"My name is Federico Golondrina.'' The stranger held out a hand. ''Are you by any chance related to the McCowans who are ranching northeast of here, beyond the valley of the Pecos?''

A frown appeared on the American's face, and he nodded. ''Yes, I am,'' he replied. ''Abigail McCowan is a cousin. Why do you ask?'' He sat up straighter on the cot, and his face took on stern lines, eyes narrowing and turning darker. ''I visited on their place only six months back, and they seemed to be doin' well. If there's trouble now, tell me about it.'' Leaning forward, he gripped the other man by the forearms, his powerful fingers biting cruelly into the flesh. A look of anguish and an involuntary cry of pain made him aware of what he was doing, and he released his grip.

"Sorry,'' he said. ''It's just that family ties are strong with us McCowans, and Abigail is special to me. Why are you here now? What have you to do with them?''

"I too have a cousin,'' the man explained. ''Carlos Montoncillo, who owns the large ranch adjoining theirs, is the son of my father's sister. Family means much to us, just as you have said, but I am not a citizen of your country, and a move by me could worsen the situation.''

McCowan stood and glared down at the Mexican. ''Damn it, man, quit beatin' around the bush and tell me what's goin' on. If there's trouble, then spit it out.''

The man held up a placating hand. ''Sit down,'' he said, shuffling the papers in his hand. ''Rancho Montoncillo is now in the hands of some men from the North, and Carlos is a prisoner in his own home. Both he and one of your cousin's sons have been gravely wounded, and many of the vaqueros on the rancho have been killed. The rest are being held, after being told that Carlos will die if they resist.''

The tall American was striding back and forth and smashing a clenched fist into his palm. "Which one?" he asked hoarsely. "Milo? The son who was just recently married?"

"No," came the reply. "One of the other sons. Lysander, I believe, is his given name. I've heard he is a veritable giant and towers far above a normal man."

"He's the youngest boy," McCowan told him. "But what of Abigail McCowan and the others? Have they been taken too?"

"I don't think so, señor. At least they weren't when I last had word. However, their ranch is under siege by those men, and they cannot leave the house, which is surrounded by heavily armed ruffians. Luckily they seem to have a goodly supply of arms and ammunition, and right now it's a Mexican standoff, as your people say.''

McCowan turned in mid-stride. "I must get out of this place. Now! Can you help me, mister?" The other man nodded, and he went on. "I'll need two good horses, both hot-blooded and able to stand the pace. I figger it's close on to three hundred miles of hard goin', but I can get there in forty-eight hours by ridin' relays.

"The constable has my revolver, and I'll need a rifle. A good one. A Henry, if you can get me one, and plenty of the cartridges it uses. A pair of saddlebags, big ones, and filled with corn for the horses. Can you do this, and quickly?''

"*Sí, señor,*" the other replied. "We can leave right now." He raised his voice for the jailer, and the door swung open. "Come! Time is of the essence, and we cannot afford to take more than necessary."

An hour later, Trace McCowan rode a big, well-muscled bay onto the north bank of the Rio Grande. In a scabbard under his leg was a brand-new Winchester, and saddlebags bulging with corn and ammunition were behind the cantle. Running alongside was an equally strong zebra dun, jealously unwilling to lag behind on the lead rope. To the west, a flaming crimson sunset sent rays across the sky, and ahead the trail stretched out toward the Pecos, and revenge.

* * *

The little frame church was filled to overflowing, and a body would have been hard put to find a place to stand, much less gain a seat. Brother Justice McCowan held up his hands in benediction as the final strains of "Where, Oh Where Are the Hebrew Children" resounded in the room.

Ex-Texas Ranger, Indian fighter, bull whacker, and now an emissary of the Lord, Justice McCowan was respected throughout the length and breadth of Texas as a sin-stompin', hellfire and damnation preacher who could reconvert the Devil himself if he just got a chance at him. Folks traveled for miles to hear him preach, and went home chastened and with full intent to lead a better life.

"Brothers and sisters," he called out. "You see here before you a sinner. A backslidin', whiskey-drinkin', devil-ridden sinner! I taken the name of the Lord in vain. Gazed with lust on my neighbor's wife. I reckon I've done broken or badly bent ever' commandment in the Good Book."

"But no more, brothers and sisters. Never again! I have seen the Light!"

"Amen!" echoed from a far corner. "Hallelujah! Praise the Lord," intoned someone from far in the back.

"Never again," continued Brother Justice, "will the taint of liquor touch my lips. Never again will I covet another man's woman. Never again will the blood of another be seen on these hands. Never again . . . What's goin' on back there? Cain't y'all see I'm full up to bustin' with them words you gotta hear, if you mean to find salvation? Who is thet feller back there thet's disturbin' the Lord's work?"

A tall skinny man, his bald pate glistening in the light from the oil lanterns, was passed through the closely packed congregation, and up to the front, where he crumpled his hat in his hands and looked up fearfully at the buckskin-clad giant towering over him.

"Well?" asked McCowan. "What's your excuse, little man?"

"Your honor, sir, I got sumpin' to tell yuh. It's your brother's daughter, sir. She's in bad trouble, an' might be kilt if help's long in comin'. It's some of them scallywag, carpetbag-carryin' no-goods from the North. They be tryin' to take over her place, sir, and there's been some shootin' already. One of her boys done been hurt, and real bad. The rider's jest outside, and he'll tell you the whole story. He sent me in to fetch yuh. I'm . . . I'm sorry, preacher!''

"Thet's all right, son." McCowan straightened, and his gaze swept over the packed room. "My sermon today was set in the Book of Leviticus and has a heap to say about lovin' our fellow man. It tells us: *Thou shalt not avenge, or bear any grudge against the children of thy people, but shalt love thy neighbor as thyself.'*

"Now, the good Lord has shown us a way to handle thet, if thy neighbor takes his hand to one of our own. In Exodus, I read: *'And if any mischief follows, then thou shalt give life for life, eye for eye, tooth for tooth,'* and so on. Right on down the line, my friends. Beware him who molests my brother's child, or her offspring. Thet's straight from the book of McCowan, and you can b'lieve ever' word!''

Reaching under the pulpit, he drew out a holstered revolver and strapped it around his waist. A hunting pouch with powder horn attached came next, and he draped it around his neck. Turning the pages of the Bible in front of him, he spoke. "Lookin' in the Book of Ephesians, we find mention of the armor of God: *'Wherefore, take unto you the whole armor of God, that ye may be able to withstand in the evil day and done all to stand . . . stand therefore, having your loins girt about with Truth.'* Now''—he patted the gunbelt—"I figger this here's my girdle of Truth, and I'm leavin' now to bring thet truth to some nonbelievers. So y'all take care now, and believe in the True Word, and mebbe whisper a leetle prayer thet this child can win through the deceivin' wiles of the trespassin' No'therners and save them as is in deep trouble now.'' He bowed his grizzled head. "Amen.''

The file of riders crossed the Red at Spanish Fort, pausing briefly to buy grain for their horses. Two young and curious cowboys approached them as they got ready to leave.

Hailing a hulking oldster who appeared to be the leader, one asked him politely, "Ain't you called Handsome Horse or somethin' like thet?"

The graying, dark-visaged man looked him over carefully. "I am called Isuba Ilafia," he replied. "And in your tongue, that does mean Handsome Horse. Why do you ask?"

The youngster looked down and stirred at the dust with a boot. "Ain't you brother to the feller thet married Abigail Mc-Cowan and had him three sons, name of Rush, Milo, and Lysander? All of 'em big fellers, jest like him?"

Several of the other riders muttered, and two reached for holstered revolvers as they moved in. The older man held up his hand and signed for them to hold up where they were.

"Yes," he replied. "I am that man. Why do you ask?"

"Well sir," the other said, "I reckon thet you must be my uncle, 'cause our daddy was her brother. Say!" He peered up at the big Indian. "You ain't got no shorter name, have you? Jest don't sound right, me callin' you Uncle Handsome Horse. Surely you got you a nickname or somethin'."

The oldster grinned, and some of his riders laughed. "I have a white man's name now, since we have moved from where we used to make our homes. I am called Frank Redman, so you can call me your uncle Frank. But tell me, what are your names, and what are you doing here in Spanish Fort?"

The youngster was grinning now. "Me? I'm Hone Mc-Cowan, and that there's my brother Hutch. We're trailin' cows for a feller name of Wheeler. Headin' on to Abilene, where the women wear paint on their faces, drink their liquor like the men, and love cowboys best of all. How about y'all, Uncle Frank? Seems like y'all's headin' south. I'm bit by the curiosity bug. What's down in Texas for you 'n' all the rest of these here fellers? You plannin' to take up land?"

The man called Frank Redman looked over at his friends. "We're riding to help your aunt Abigail and her sons. Some men from the North have badly wounded your cousin Lysander and are trying to kill the rest of the family. I'm not sure why they are doing this, but we're going to find out soon."

The boy looked over at his brother, and they both nodded.

"Well, then I reckon we'll jest trail along with y'all. I guess I'd better tell Wheeler, so's he can hire two more drovers. Y'all go on ahead. We'll ketch up right soon."

Port Isabel, Texas, is a small, open anchorage and a port of entry for much of the goods coming out of Old Mexico. Less than ten years ago many optimists heading out for the California goldfields were still using it for a jumping-off place.

This particular morning it was a battered lugger holding the attention of the few idlers on the pier—or more strictly speaking, the big sunburnt man in bleached, chopped-off cotton pants who was tying her up. Lank black hair hung a couple of inches down his muscular back, and his bare feet left wet tracks on the splintered planks of the rickety pier. Aware of the stares, his big white teeth showed in a grin.

"As you can no doubt perceive," he announced, "I am more needful of a suit of clothes than even a hearty meal, and I would be in your debt if you could direct me to the nearest clothing store. Not," he continued, "that I wouldn't enjoy a large, juicy beefsteak with all the trimmings. But I would enjoy such a repast even more if I were suitably togged out. Come now, surely one of you gentlemen can speak."

One of the spectators roused himself long enough to point a hand in a northerly direction and mumble something to the effect of: "Second street over and you'll see the sign."

With a wave of thanks the nearly naked man reached down and took a ragged blanket roll out of the boat and set on a course for the direction indicated. Ten minutes later, with a big smile on his bronzed face, he entered the store of Abe Feathermann and stated his wants.

Seemingly unconcerned by the stranger's unusual garb, the middle-aged proprietor helped him to select his choice, then escorted him to an alcove separated from the main shop by a pair of blankets hung from a wire.

"You'll need boots, young man," Feathermann stated. "But that can wait until you've tried the suit. If the fit will require alteration, I can accomplish that in a few minutes."

"Right now," came the reply, "I could sure use something

to eat. Not a complete meal, but rather something to nibble on. I'm afraid I haven't had much of anything for upward of a week now, and my stomach is protesting loudly.''

''I have a chicken stewing on the stove in back,'' the shop owner told him. ''You see, I'm an unmarried man, and my home is in the rear of this building. It's not much to offer to a gentleman such as yourself, but I'd be happy to share with you. Come now. Hurry into the suit, and follow me into the back. It's just about my lunchtime anyway, and I'll put a sign on the door.''

The chicken *was* good, and the stranger more than did justice to his share. Some fresh-baked bread and strong sour wine completed their meal, and Feathermann brought out a box of long thin cigars, offering one to his guest.

''Say, Mr. Feathermann, I want to tell you how much I've enjoyed this meal, but I can't seem to find the words. Will I be offending you if I offer to pay for your kindness to a complete stranger?'' The big man laughed.

''Hadn't really thought about it, but I would imagine that you've been wondering if I *could* pay. I mean, wandering in here half naked, with nothing on but a pair of ragged old pants. But I can pay, and handsomely. That is, if I can find someone who knows gems. You see, I have no cash money. Just some very excellent diamonds.'' He reached down, fumbling with the rawhide ties on his blanket roll, which he had brought along into the rear of the building.

''Please,'' the older man told him, ''call me Abe; everyone hereabouts does. By pure coincidence I deal in both stones and precious metals. Much comes through this little hole-in-the-wall port that isn't common knowledge, and I learned to take advantage of whatever is offered. Come. Show me those diamonds of which you speak.'' He reached into a vest pocket and took out a glass, which he fitted into one eye.

Minutes later he looked up in awe. ''Why, you have the makings of a fortune here, my boy! Where did you find gems like these beauties? They are simply fantastic stones.''

The smile on the stranger's face faded, and he considered for an instant before replying. ''Venezuela,'' he told his questioner. "Up the Orinoco River, and into the Guiana Highlands. It began as a lark, and we had no idea we would find anything like this. There were three of us—myself, plus two of my friends from college. I'm the only survivor." An anguished frown flashed across his face.

"We stumbled on these by accident. Matter of fact, much more than you see here. Like fools, we announced our fortunate find to the local authorities and found ourselves held prisoner in a filthy dungeon moments later."

Abe Feathermann smiled tolerantly. "There's no reason for playing games, mister. What did you say your name was, young man?"

"McCowan." Another smile. "Mahlon McCowan. I guess I didn't fool you for a minute, did I?"

"Young man," Feathermann replied, "diamonds are not normally found in the jungles of South America with facets cut so precisely. As a matter of fact, they look more like some of the water-washed moonstones you can find on any beach."

"Yeah, I see what you mean, Mr. Feathermann. Anyway, do you wish to buy the stones? If not, can you lend me enough so I *can* find a buyer? I seem to be without any funds just now, and I would like to pay you for your kindness and this suit. You can keep one of the stones as collateral, and we will consider it a regular business agreement. Along with a pair of boots, I'll need socks, shirts, and a hat, of course. Oh, yes! These diamonds may prove a temptation for someone, and I'd better invest in a belt gun of some sort."

The merchant smiled indulgently. In spite of the fact that the gems were obviously stolen, he was certain that the young man seated across the table would not have taken the diamonds unless there was some justification. Perhaps his theft had been from someone high in the government. A ruthless tyrant who had obtained them illegally himself. What a pity that he would never know the real story. He envied and resented the other's daring, but he *would* buy the gems.

"I believe we can agree on a price. These are very fine and valuable diamonds. I won't ask where they do come from, but

I'm depending on you to assure me that the rightful owner will not be around later to claim them.

"By the way, Mr. McCowan, do you by chance have some relatives in southwest Texas? Say, along the military road leading to El Paso? I believe the lady's name is Abigail; a ranch called the CMC Connected. She has three sons, one who is called Lightly."

"Why, yes! She's my father's only sister. A real fine old lady, and the apple of my daddy's eye. Why do you ask?"

"Because the word is out that some enterprising businessmen from the North have her place under siege right now. I believe one son is either dead or dying, and another cannot be reached. . . ." Feathermann's voice faltered. "Wait! What is wrong, McCowan? If I've offended . . .''

The big man's smile was really gone this time. He looked grim, and his eyes burned into the shopkeeper's.

"Pay me what you wish for the stones," he rasped. "I got urgent business, and not much time! I'll want two ten-gauge double guns, a hacksaw, and some latigo thongs. A real fast horse'd come in handy, and I'd appreciate you telling me the shortest, fastest road to the Val Verde."

The woman in the feathered hat was indignant. The tall man had brushed past her without so much as an apology and strode through the door, leaving behind the scent of pungent wood smoke, horse sweat, and leather clothing that, strangely enough, set her pulse to racing. She watched as he loosened his horse's reins and swung up into the saddle, riding out of her life forever. She sighed and turned to the grocer.

"Who was he?" she asked. "He seemed so angry and intent on leaving. Why, he almost knocked me off my feet!"

The merchant stood there watching as the rider rode out of sight. In his hand he held two gold coins, payment for the food and ammunition the man had purchased. Recognition and nervous fear had set his knees to knocking, and now he hardly remembered a word of their conversation. Most of the man's talk had been perfunctory until the grocer had spoken of the Val Verde affair, in a foolish attempt to shatter the man's infuriating calm. Now, turning to the woman, he tried to keep his voice steady.

"That there was Cass McCowan, ma'am. He's a killer, Miss Emily, and a wanted man. He's headed for the Val Verde, and more killing. God have mercy on anybody gets in his way!"

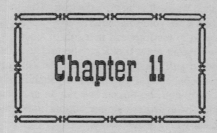

Chapter 11

A timid-sounding tap came at the door, and Esperanza rose to her feet with eyebrows raised. *"Quién es?"* she asked. *"Es Lupe, señorita. Está un hombre malo aquí que quiere hablar con usted y el señor también. Ahora, señorita!"*

Before Esperanza could explain that it was her maid who had knocked, we heard a gruff voice telling the girl to move away from the door, and suddenly it swung open and we saw two men standing in the doorway. One was that officer who'd slashed me with the saber. He bowed politely to Esperanza. Favoring me with a curt nod, he spoke.

"I am here at the request of Mr. Gresham to invite both of you to dinner this evening. Provided, that is, McCowan is suf-

ficiently recovered to leave his bed.'' He paused and gazed
speculatively around the room. ''My,'' he said, ''you've certainly shown a creative taste, Miss Montoncillo. I can't remember when I've seen a more beautifully done room. These
furnishings blend perfectly with the dark-beamed ceiling and
the whitewashed walls. It is an effective use of the local materi-
als, and a credit to your ingenuity.'' He bowed again and
touched his hand to his forehead in a sort of salute.

''Dinner will be at eight o'clock,'' he told us. ''By then it
will have cooled sufficiently that we can be comfortably relaxed and more congenial. I've found heat negates calm.'' One
hand on the doorknob, he turned and ran an appreciative eye
over Esperanza, who wore a simple cotton frock and had her
hair drawn back with a white cloth.

''I hope you will see fit to wear something appropriate to the
occasion, Miss Montoncillo. It is seldom that we in the field are
privileged to enjoy the company of a lovely woman. Especially
one so obviously mature as you.'' Again he bowed, then left,
closing the door behind him.

Esperanza turned, and we stared at each other—me with a
mixed feeling of anger and amazement, and her with some consternation. Naturally I resented the way he had ogled over Esperanza, though I couldn't blame him. She *was* lovely, and
carried herself like the thoroughbred I knew her to be.

''Are these fellers crazy, or are we?'' I asked. ''Here we are,
prisoners in your pa's house, me with my head slashed open
and my arm almost cut off, and they're sendin' invites to dinner.'' I thought a moment. ''How come they're eatin' the noon
meal at eight o'clock at night? Our evenin' meal's usually
called supper. Thet proves they're all mixed up.''

Esperanza explained that back east, in polite company, it was
proper to call the evening meal dinner. ''At midday a light
lunch is served,'' she told me.

''Well,'' I told her, ''whatever they got in mind for us, I
would bet hard money it ain't somethin' we're gonna enjoy.''

Esperanza stared at me. ''Aren't you the least bit worried?''
she asked. ''Here we are being held prisoner by some men we
don't even know! Not only that, but we have no idea why they

are here or what they plan to do with us. We could be killed, and no one would be the wiser. Doesn't the prospect of dying worry you? Don't you have some plans? An idea of some kind? A plan for getting us out of here along with my father? We can't just sit back like a pair of dummies and let these men do whatever they wish with us!'' She looked like tears might come any minute, and I was quick to comfort her.

''C'mere, honey.'' I reached out a hand, and she taken it. ''First off I got a question or two to ask you, then we'll talk over what can be done. You said I'd been unconscious a week or more. I can see I've lost some weight, but I don't seem to be overly hungry or thirsty right now. How in heck did you manage to git water and food into me? You must have given me something, else I'd be weaker'n I am. Why . . .'' The full impact of what she must have had to do suddenly came.

''Why, you must have had . . . you had to . . . you taken the care of me that a mother does for her child. Plumb unconscious, I was helpless to do for myself, and you did it all. Honey, I thank you. That's about all I *can* do right now. But you can bet your last peso I'm gonna spend the rest of my life jest makin' this up to you. I love you, Esperanza, and will go on lovin' you forever. I'm glad you waited until I was able to come along. It'd break my heart to see you married to somebody else.''

She knelt down by the bed and kissed me tenderly. ''You are the only man in the world for me, Lyse. I love you more each day and yearn for the time when we can be together. I know that you will find a way out of this for us and all of the others. They are *our* responsibility now, since my father has closed himself off from all of us.''

I patted her shoulder. ''Don't you be frettin' yourself about Don Carlos. He's powerful strong. Look at how he has overcome bein' crippled! He jest refused to let it slow him down, and did somethin' about it. He ain't no quitter. The grief always comes first, but anger ain't never far behind.''

As I laid there with her head on my shoulder, I got me a-thinking about what *could* be done. First off, I figgered, I had best see if I could stand on my own two feet. So with that in mind I asked Esperanza to bring me my clothes. "It ain't right," I told her. "Me bein' here alone with you in this room, and us not married and all. If I can walk, then I'm gonna ask them fellers if I can't bunk with your pa, or mebbe in with Vargas. Thet captain, he'll understand, and I reckon I'll jest send for him. You know, there's one thing thet really bothers me. Why am I still alive? Why would he not finish the job? He had a pretty fair start, what with a slash to the face like thet. Far's thet goes, why not jest let me bleed to death? They had good cause, after me flingin' their top man halfway across the room. I sure enough couldn't help myself, seein' poor little Poco Luce lyin' in a pool of blood, with thet cocked eye of his starin' off into nowhere. There was more pure-D guts and grit packed into thet little feller than a man twice his size. I'm not gonna forget him. You can bank on thet."

While I was jabbering away, Esperanza had gone ahead and gotten my clothes out of her wardrobe. She laid them on the bed near to hand. "I'll just sit over there in the chair, Lyse, with my back turned. That is, unless you think you'll need help in getting out of bed. I'd be happy to help out in any way I can." There was a mischievous look about her, and I couldn't help but grin. She smiled. "After all," she said, "your body is no secret to me." She laughed, and that taken away my embarrassment somehow, and I joined in after a moment's hesitation.

"Thanks anyway, honey. If I cain't git outta bed without help, I doubt I'd be much on walkin' anywhere. Don't be too uppity, Miss Montoncillo. You ain't so big I cain't be turnin' you over my knee. Remember thet. Honestly, I really feel pretty good, all things considered. My head aches some, and this arm pains me a little, but I'll be jest fine. Hard to hurt an old mountain boy like me."

Soon as she was settled in her chair, I snagged my underwear and drew it on. Had some trouble one-handing the buttons, but finally managed to get the job done. The rest was fairly easy, and in no time at all I was fully dressed, except for drawing on my boots.

"You can look now," I told her. "Might not be such a bad

idea if you was to come and hang on to me, while I see if my legs'll hold me up. I do feel sorta light-headed.''

"It's no wonder," she said. "All you've had to eat since you were hurt was the sugar water and beef broth I managed to spoon into your mouth. I know how much food you normally put away. You're a big man, and it takes a lot to fill you. You'll feel much better after you've eaten some solid food. Believe me.''

With her help I managed to stand. I was some wobbly, in spite of my determination not to be, but that only lasted no more'n the first few minutes. Soon I was walking the full length of the room and back without help. Reaching over, I taken my hat and tried to fit it on over the bandage. It wasn't possible, so I gave up and hung the hat on the rack.

"Reckon I'll have them send for the captain now," I told her. "But first I'd like the lend of a mirror. It'll likely scare me half to death, 'cause no man lies in bed for over a week, sick like I was, without he looks like death warmed over. I'm sure I ain't no exception, but I jest gotta have a look-see.'' She brought me a mirror with a fancy silvered frame and held it up for me.

I hardly recognized the gaunt, hollow-cheeked stranger in the glass. My eyes seemed sunk halfway into my head, and my overlarge nose jutted out like a tomahawk blade. Pale, and stretched tight over the cheekbones, my face had a few long hairs sprouting like weeds in an untended garden.

"Lucky for me I'm mostly Injun," I told her. "Otherwise I'd have a pretty good growth of beard to shave off. In the old days, or so Paw told us boys, our folks used to consider hair on a man's face ugly, and agin nature. Fast as it appeared, they'd pluck out the hair, usin' clam shells like a pair of tweezers. After a time the hair plumb gave up.''

Using my fingers, I gave each one a quick yank, and soon the hairs were gone. Smarted some, but I figgered it better than going around looking like some old Chinaman. I didn't envy the fellers who had to use a razor every day, although I had to admit some men did look fine wearing a full beard.

"Before I talk to the guard," I told Esperanza, "I figger

you'd best hang on to this derringer. They wouldn't think to search you, and you can always pass it over to me if we git in a spot where we can use it. I'm jest hopin' thet feller I taken it from won't remember to ask for it.

"Here." I handed her the little gun, and the three extra cartridges. "You never can tell. Thet might jest give us the edge we'll need. With it I can mebbe git me a guard's gun and shoot our way outta here if we have to."

"It's your time to turn around," she told me. "I believe that my garter will hold the derringer very well, and those cartridges I'll keep in my dress pocket. But first, please show me how this operates. It might be me who has to disarm the guard, and I want to be able to shoot if necessary."

Quickly I showed her how the barrel was released by the large button catch on the right side of the frame. "Press this back after you set the hammer at half-cock." I demonstrated as I spoke. "Then the barrel will move a quarter turn to the right and can be loaded or unloaded. Once the cartridge is in the chamber, turn the barrel back and it'll lock in place. Bring the hammer to full-cock and by pressing the trigger the gun will fire. Don't even try to shoot somebody at any distance. This little gun's best range is a few feet, and does a better job jammed into the belly. Git close in behind and stick it under an ear. You'll make believers outta most anybody, and they'll do most anything you ask. I'm hopin' you never have to use it, but you might.

"Well, here goes. I'm hopin' they'll let me bunk with your pa, and thet way I can mebbe cheer him up, or at least git him mad enough so's he'll fight back. Wish me luck. I reckon I'll need all I can git, honey."

She reached up and put her arms around my neck. "This is so you won't forget what you're fighting for, Lyse. I'm praying for us all." With that she kissed me on the mouth, and I'll bet that was the longest kiss ever. My old heart got to pounding until it liken to jumped outta my chest. I could feel the warm softness of her through the thin dress, and I could hardly breathe. Gently I loosed her arms from around my neck and stepped back a pace.

"I'm sorry, honey," I told her. "Thet's too much like us lightin' a fuse, and we had better wait for a spell. Much more of thet and I won't be wantin' to go anywhere."

Going to the door, I tried the knob and found it locked, so I rapped hard with my knuckles.

"Yeah? What d'ye want?" The guard sounded bored.

"I'd like to talk with thet captain feller," I came back. "How's about you huntin' him up? It's important."

"Well, I dunno," came his reply. "He's easy riled, and I don't wanna get in no trouble. What d'ye wanna talk about?"

"You jest tell him thet it's about the young lady and a little privacy. He'll understand, and he won't git mad. You can bet on thet. C'mon now, before I decide to kick in this here door. Git goin' now and see if you can hunt him up."

"Huh! You try kickin' in that door and you'll be sorry. I'll put a Spencer ball in your guts, and you can bet on it, bucko. I got my orders, and there ain't nothin' says I have to take a lotta guff off of you." He didn't sound all that certain, so I asked again, this time a bit more politely.

"C'mon, soldier. Give this young lady a break, will you? She's been cooped up in this here room for more'n a week."

"Well . . ." He still sounded uncertain. "I guess maybe the captain won't mind. I'll do like you asked, but I warn you, there's another sentry right down the hall, so don't you be tryin' to kick down that door whilst I'm gone. He'll shoot you down and ask the questions after."

We heard him holler to the other guard, and then he left, his footsteps growing fainter as he moved down the hall. I turned to Esperanza. "I don't think you'll have to worry—about the captain, that is. He's attracted, but I figger he considers himself too much the gentleman to take advantage. If he feels like talkin' after they've taken me away, you'd be wise to listen. He might jest give us a clue as to what they plan on doin' here. Meantimes I'll see what I can do to git your pa's dander up. Make him mad enough to help us run these fellers plumb out of Texas, or bury 'em here."

She nodded and gave me a quick kiss. "I'll try my best, Lyse. It won't be easy, because I can't stand that captain.

When he looked at me, it was like he could see right through my dress. I'm not so sure that he'll stay at arm's length, especially if he feels I'm responding to him.''

I nodded soberly. "If it comes to thet, sweetheart, I want you to go ahead and use thet derringer on him. However it turns out, we'll make do. Like I said earlier, the fact thet one of them vaqueros got away means thet help could be comin' anytime now. There's still the four men at Sycamore Canyon camp. If he rides there—and I'm fairly certain that he would—then we have five men out there. Plus thet Apache cook,'' I added. "Between them they can cover a lot of territory, lookin' for help.''

Approaching footsteps warned us the guard was coming back to the room. Sounded like more'n one man, so I figgered the captain must be along. I gave Esperanza a pat on the shoulder and faced the door as the key turned in the lock.

It *was* the captain, and he had a questioning look on his face. "Whatever you have to say, McCowan, say it fast. Our plans include you, but you aren't indispensable. Believe me. Myself, I wouldn't feel too bad had you died from the saber cut. Any man your size is dangerous to keep around.''

To my credit, I remained as polite as possible. "Reason I had to see you, Cap'n, was to ask a favor. Miss Esperanza hasn't had any privacy for more'n a week now. She's never really had any proper rest because of worryin' about me. I was wonderin', wouldn't it be better all around if some other quarters could be found for me? That would give her a chance to rest and freshen up for tonight. Way things are, she can't even dress in private. Besides, it ain't proper, the two of us bein' in here together. Was one thing while I was sick and unconscious, but now it's a different story.''

He looked me over, shrewdly, like he was reading my mind. "McCowan, Are you certain that this is your only reason for wanting to be moved? Myself, I would certainly welcome this type of arrangement.'' He looked meaningfully toward Esperanza with a sly smile on his thin, bony face.

Right then I wanted to grab him by his skinny neck, lift him off the floor, and choke the life out of him. I promised I would do just that, and soon. Trying to keep the anger from showing too plainly, I went on.

"I figgered mebbe I could be put in with Don Carlos, so's I could help him git around. He's plumb crippled, you know, and since you've killed his servant, he's helpless. I heard he ain't eatin' enough to keep a bird alive, and that's real bad. In his condition he could sicken to a point where he jest might die. Then where would you fellers be? You'd be missin' a hostage, mebbe the most important one of us all."

He wasn't smiling anymore, and appeared worried. Seemed like mebbe I'd hit the nail right on the head, I mused. The only reason for keeping any of us alive was sorta obvious, I reckoned. If it wasn't for hostages, and the threat of them being killed, our rancher neighbors could band together and wipe out these marauding deserters, or whatever they were.

That was another thing that bothered me. We'd been on a friendly basis with the troops at Camp Hudson before they'd packed up and pulled out, leaving few behind. Their doctor had tended to Milo last year when he'd been shot up by the Shaler gang. Rush had saved Lieutenant O'Dowd's bacon one time in Juno, and both O'Dowd and Doc Weisel had broke bread with us at the ranch, and even slept over. Though they'd considered us McCowans Johnny Rebs, we'd never had any trouble with the Union soldiers. Why were we being bothered now, and why would they even consider harming the Montoncillos?

The officer was staring at the rafters and fiddling with the hilt of his sword, apparently deep in thought. Glancing at his collar, I saw the letters MV pinned next to crossed sabers and asked him the meaning of the insignia.

"Hmmm? What was that?" Lost in thought, he was startled by my question. I pointed at his collar tabs.

"Those letters on your collar? What do they stand for?"

He stared at me, and his glance wasn't all that friendly. "It's really none of your affair," he told me. "But it can't really matter at this point. Missouri Volunteers. We were all volunteers, and ready to give our lives for our country. Not our fault that some fat-bellied general in Washington chose to keep us always in reserve. But enough of that!"

Apparently the captain had made up his mind. He motioned to a guard, a short feller who ran mostly to fat. "Take this man over to the living quarters of Don Carlos," he told him. "Watch him carefully, and don't hesitate to shoot if he makes any attempt to get away. Ask one of the other men to accompany you, and give him the same instructions. If he even *looks* like he's trying to escape, put a ball into him. I will stay here and have a few words with the young lady."

Esperanza made signs that she'd be all right, but I wondered. I knew she had the derringer, and I was sure that it would do the job if she really needed it. Still, I wondered—would she actually shoot if it came to that? Shooting another human being wasn't easy for anyone, and I wasn't sure she'd be able to do that, even when her own life was in danger. Wasn't anything I could do, so I followed the guard out of the room and down the hall, with the other one close behind, his rifle muzzle in the middle of my back.

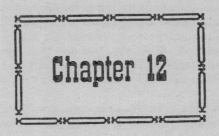

Chapter 12

Carlos had his living quarters on the main floor, back in a corner. As we came to his door I'd swear I heard a sorta scuffling noise, and it came from inside. Neither one of my guards seemed to hear it, or if they did, didn't really care about it one way or the other. One of them knocked, but he didn't wait for an answer. Just opened the door and called out, "Hey, Don whatchumacallit! We got some comp'ny, and it's that feller McCowan. Ain't yuh gonna come here to the door and say hello?"

"Hell," the other man told him. "You know damn well the man's a cripple. I ain't no angel, but I sure don't mock an old man that's got no legs under him. You'd best watch for lightning to strike, bucko. There's some things a man don't wanna ever say, else he'll git in the same fix someday.''

"G'wan in," the other said. He prodded me with the rifle barrel, and I stumbled inside, still feeling light-headed.

"*Donde estás, Don Carlos?*" I asked. "Where are you? I'm not seein' too well after bein' out in the bright sunlight. It'll take my eyes a minute to git adjusted to the dark."

"Is it really you, Lysander?" He seemed mighty relieved, somehow, and I wondered why. Had they been abusing him? Was the one guard's sarcasm typical of the way he'd been treated by these men? Surely they wouldn't think of hurting him!

"Sure it's me, Carlos. Where are you, anyway? It's sort of dark in here with the blinds drawn. Feller could easily break his neck stumblin' over the furniture." It *was* a big room—actually two rooms, connected by an archway. Bedroom and *sala,* or drawing room, in which Carlos had his desk and did all his book work. I'd only been in the place once. Last year, when we'd come back from Abilene, I'd brought Carlos's share of the herd money to him. We'd spent most half a day with him asking questions and me telling about the drive.

"Are you alone?" he asked. "Have those men gone, or have they stayed to eavesdrop on our conversation?"

"Far as I know, they're gone," I told him. "But you wait. They locked the door, but they could be standing outside."

My eyes were gradually adjusting to the gloom. As yet I still hadn't located Carlos, but I saw a tray of food on the table near the door, and it didn't look like much of it had been eaten. Esperanza had been right, it seemed. He wasn't eating as much as he should, and that sure wasn't like him.

"I'm over here, Lysander. Here on the floor, beside this bed of mine. I'll need a lift up, if you don't mind. Somewhat embarrassing to admit it, but I'm not able to raise myself to the height of the bed. Leave the blinds drawn, as a favor to me. I have a reason, and you will understand."

I fumbled my way past the furniture and found him on the floor, just as he'd said. He sure wasn't no lightweight, no, sir! Pushing two hundred pounds or more! I wondered how a skinny little feller like Poco Luce ever got him off and on his horse, but I'd seen him do it many's the time.

Once I'd got him up on the bed I pushed a couple pillows in behind his back and he was able to sit up by himself. A look of concern was on his face as he noticed the bandages wrapped around my head and covering my left arm.

"How are you feeling, Lysander? Are your wounds healing as they should? To tell the truth, I'd forgotten about your bad arm. I should never have asked you to lift me, with the arm so badly injured."

To be honest, I'd really felt the pain while lifting him to the bed, but I lied a little bit and said he really didn't weigh all that much.

"What the heck were you doin' on the floor, Carlos? Were you jest crawlin', or did you fall? Why didn't you give out a holler or somethin'? I didn't see no guard at your door, but surely somebody would have heard you if you'd hollered loud and long enough."

He signed for me to bend down closer and whispered, "I want you to go to the door quietly and make certain nobody is listening. I have something to tell you, and no one else must hear what I have to say. Hurry now!"

I did just that. There was a small barred opening in the center of the door, about five feet off the floor, and I was able to see pretty well. The two guards who had walked me to his room were about twenty feet away, both with pipes in their mouths and deep in conversation.

Moving to a window, I made sure no one was leaning on the wall next to the door, then went back to Carlos. "Seems we don't have nobody interested in us, amigo. The guards can't hear us. They're too far away. Now what is it you wanted to tell me that's so secret?"

"*Mucho*, my young friend. Enough that we can spend hours in conversation and yet leave much untold. But first let me tell you the *good* news." His eyes were sparkling, and he looked like he might bust out laughing any minute.

"Have you perhaps wondered," he asked me, "where Lancelot Gilkie might be? Whether or not he was able to escape

when these *cabrones* invaded my home? You haven't? Well, I
don't wonder, Lysander. After all, if what I've been told is the
truth, you have only recently awakened from a coma, a result of
the head wound you suffered. But no matter.

"Do you remember the *baile* last year? The dance and the fi-
esta to which I'd invited your family? If so, then you'd remember the small room in the patio wall where we had the
Winchesters stored, and the revolvers that shoot six times."

"Sure," I told him. "Miguel Vargas showed me, and I taken
Rush in there so's he could see all them guns. How could I
forgit somethin' like thet? I'd never seen so many brand-new
guns in my life."

He was smiling broadly now. "If you recall," he said to me,
"the door to that room was concealed in the wall. It was impossible to see the door, or to open it, if you didn't know the loca-
tion of the secret lever. Am I not right?"

"Yes." I nodded. "But what has thet to do with Gilkie?"

"Because"—he was shaking with glee—"because he is *in*
that room right at this very moment." He reached for my arm.
"Not only that," he said, "but there is a passage in the wall of
this room that leads to that one. When you appeared with the
two guards, Lancelot Gilkie was right here talking with me.
That's why the blinds are drawn, and that, also, is why I
wanted to know if you were alone."

"Well, I'll be a . . . Then you have a plan, Carlos? Some
way that we can beat these devils and git your place back?"

His face fell. "No, Lysander, not really a plan. That room,
and the fact that Gilkie is free, may help a lot, but I haven't
thought out a plan as yet. There are things we know nothing
about. The total number of men under their command, both
here and at your family's ranch. Then, too, I would want to be
certain that we could kill or capture the leaders early in our attempt. Without someone to give them orders and guarantee
their pay, these *cabrones* would merely ride out of here, and
we'll have won the battle."

I found myself opening and closing my fists, wishing that I
had that death's-head of a captain where I could throttle the life
out of him. I was afraid for Esperanza, although I knew she had

the little gun to protect her. With all of his men to help him, he could do almost anything he wanted with her—or with any of us, for that matter. 'Course, having old man Gilkie free to help us really made a difference. Gilkie was a freed slave, one hell of a man, and one of the finest, most imaginative trail-driving cooks I'd ever met. His son, a young cowboy of eighteen or so, had been killed on a drive we'd made last year. Gilkie was a real battler, and I never knew him to back down to no man.

Either Carlos was reading my thoughts or my expressions, because his next question concerned Esperanza. I told him a little of what had taken place before they'd brought me. "I figgered if you 'n' I could git our heads together, Carlos, we jest might come up with some kind of answer to the problem." Then another thought came to me.

"Are there any guns left in thet room?" I asked him. "If we could git a hold of some arms, mebbe we could make a stab at takin' over. I'll tell you what. Tonight, whilst me 'n' Esperanza's sittin' down to supper with these fellers, I'll sorta size 'em up, and mebbe I can come up with some kind of plan. Main thing, I reckon, is gittin' them vaqueros loose so's they can help out, and thet ain't gonna be easy. Without 'em we don't stand a chance, but if we can arm them all with Winchesters, we'll show these fellers a thing or two."

Carlos was shaking his head. "I'm sorry, Lysander. We distributed those rifles to the servants. There may be four or five left in the storeroom, but not enough to do much for us. These fellows are apparently well trained, and they are certainly well armed, now that they have our rifles."

One thing had been really bothering me, and now I felt it was time to ask. "Jest how did these fellers git in here, Carlos? Like you said before, this place is built strong as any fort, and you had enough men to defend it. How come you couldn't fight 'em off? Did they trick you?"

He taken a moment before answering my question. After staring across the room, a bitter smile on his face, he made up his mind and began to talk. "Late in the afternoon, the men in the towers reported a large party of mounted men approaching. We armed everyone and gave them each fifty of the Winchester cartridges. Sanchez commanded those who were defending the walls, and Gilkie organized ten men who could ride into a mounted force, one that could strike anywhere, when help was needed in a hurry. They remained close to the corrals, where they could guard our rear.

"As the riders came nearer, we could see that they had on the uniform of the United States, and their leader was wearing the bars of a captain. Riding next to him was that fat pig in civilian clothing and the deputy U.S. marshal who's not exactly friendly to our cause. When they were within no more than fifty *varas* of the gate, Sanchez called on them to halt and asked them to state their business here. He also explained that the ranch was private property and told them that they were trespassing."

"Well, what did they say to thet?" I asked. "Didn't they know about your agreement with the commander at Camp Hudson? He promised this ranch would be off-limits to soldiers."

Carlos held up his hand. "Please," he said. "The telling of how I was such a fool isn't easy for me, so be patient and let me continue my story." I nodded and listened carefully as he went on.

"The captain was very polite, and asked only if his men's canteens could be filled and their horses watered. He said their destination was Camp Hudson, and they were tired after what had been a long ride. I saw no reason to refuse, so we opened the gates and allowed them to ride in. I instructed my servants to put away their rifles, and sent one to Gilkie with word that everything was all right. Moments later the captain showed his true colors. He drew his revolver and pointed it at me, saying that he would shoot me dead if any of my men resisted." He paused for a moment, and it was obvious to me that he was close to tears.

"I'd forgotten about Poco Luce. Maybe if I'd told him to lay down his rifle he would still be alive. When he saw me threatened with the captain's revolver, he literally went berserk. His first shot struck the pistol and tore it from the officer's hand. Then he levered shots from his carbine so fast it sounded like one of those rapid-fire guns. Shot at every man in the room, and killed at least five, or so we were told later on.

"Myself, I don't really know what happened, because I was hit by one of the bullets aimed at Poco Luce. It was only a grazing wound," he hastened to assure me, "but it caused me to lose consciousness. When I awakened I found him dead on the floor, still clutching his beloved Winchester, with that poor, cocked eye staring off into space."

"Don't blame yourself," I told him. "Poco Luce died with a smile on his face. What better way to go than to die defendin' someone you love? Mebbe wherever he is now he can look down here, with both eyes straight, and know he did his best. Right now we gotta worry about the livin', and first on our list is takin' back this here ranch from these bandit fellers. Now, what'd Gilkie have in mind?"

Carlos smiled ruefully. "Like you, he is very anxious to fight them, but he is older, and perhaps wiser. He knows the odds are against us, but he's still willing to try. You can talk with him this evening, after most of our guards are asleep. I've asked him to ascertain how many guns there are in the hidden room, and also how many cartridges. I'm still afraid the odds are too great, Lysander. These men will not be easy to defeat."

"Well then," I told him, "we'll jest have to depend on a surprise of some kind. If we can take 'em a few at a time, then we'll use their own guns against them. Main thing, far as I can see, is to keep our eyes open. Wait for them soldiers to git careless, and then hit 'em hard." I looked over the room as best I could. Even though my eyes had gotten a little adjusted to the gloom, I still couldn't see too well.

"Whereabouts can a man wash his face 'n' hands, Carlos? If I'm gonna sit down to eat with them fellers, I'd jest as soon be cleaned up, with my hair combed."

Carlos pointed out a pitcher and basin over in a corner and suggested I open the blind for more light. "There's the mirror," he told me. "Right over the washstand. The water I use comes from a spring behind the corral. We bring it here through a pipe that leads to a tank on the roof. Just turn the tap and you'll find the water is warm. It's one of the few luxuries I allow myself. The sun does the work for us, although I believe it would do a better job if we fashioned a network of pipes on the roof, one in which the water could stand in greater quantity and furnish enough to bathe.''

I opened the tap, as he suggested, and marveled at what I found. Imagine! Warm, running water inside the house! The flow was steady, but not too warm, and I wasted no time getting myself clean again. The cabin I'd put up on the ranch I had started for Rush and myself was close to water. Sure wasn't no reason I couldn't do just as Carlos had done. My original idea had been for Rush and me to share the cabin, at least until the spread really got on a paying basis. Now I had to change my planning. Esperanza would be living in our new home, and we'd have to build an add-on, when and if Rush ever came back to the Val Verde. Far as that went, we'd not be waiting for Rush's return, chances were. That is, if our marriage was blessed with children early on. A cradle over in a corner would do for a time, but eventually we'd have to build rooms for the kids. Boy, I thought to myself, this is really dreaming on a grand scale!

Right now my two adopted cousins, Pak and Tunk Mc-Cowan, were building a bunkhouse for themselves and the new hands that would come with a successful ranch. Leastways, I hoped they were. I'd left 'em hard at work when I started toward town. How long back was that? Seemed like a month or more now, but I knew it was only a week. So much had happened!

Both youngsters, they were really no blood kin. In fact, they were two Kiowa boys whose uncle had talked Rush into taking them along on last year's drive to Abilene. Their uncle, who was a main chief of the Kiowa, felt that their chances would be far better if they learned the cow business. Their real names were Pak-onk-ya, or Black Buffalo, and Tunk-aht-oh-ye, meaning the Thunderer. Rush had concocted the story of them being cousins of ours from back in Kentucky, and had shortened their names for convenience. When we got back from Abilene, they'd decided to stick with me, and it'd worked out fine.

Drying my hands and face, I made a decision. I'd never say a

word about the running water to Esperanza. Just go on and
bring water to a tank on the roof, like they'd managed to do
here, and it'd be a real surprise to my bride. The cabin was built
at the foot of a bench, and with my flowing, year-round spring
high above, it would be so easy to do.

Bending down from my height, I peered in the mirror. I'd
unwrapped the bandage from my head, and the raw, ugly
wound made by the captain's saber was not easy to look at.
Scars were nothing new to me, and I had my share. Knocking
around farms and ranches, a feller'd naturally get hurt now and
again. I had a doozie on one shin, where a big calf had tore off a
patch of skin while I was wrestling him down. But I had to admit this one was different. Maw'd always said I'd inherited my
paw's good looks, along with his size and great strength. She
allowed as how I was the pick of her litter, but she'd never feel
that way now. The ragged wound started just above my left ear,
and ran down almost to my chin.

Esperanza had done a good job sewing me up, but I'd sure be
packing this one for the rest of my natural life. I had my doubts.
How would she feel about me when she saw that ugly, disfigur-
ing mark on my face? How could a lovely girl like Esperanza
settle for a lifetime of staring at me? The thought sort of taken
the heart out of me.

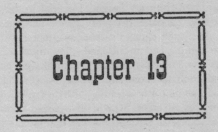

Chapter 13

Dirty and dog-tired, Trace McCowan made his first camp at dusk the third night running. Both he and the horses were near played out, and he'd been rubbing tobacco grains in his eyes for some time now, trying to stay awake. Switching the saddle every three hours, he'd been constantly on the trail since leaving Ojinaga. At a lope or a running walk he had slowly closed the miles separating him from his destination, pausing only briefly to grain and water the horses sparingly as he washed down hardtack biscuits with water from his dwindling supply and chewed jerky on the run. Now he knew he was close. A saw-toothed ridge rearing starkly in the fading light was recognizable as one visible from the ranch of Cousin Abigail. From here on he would need daylight.

He had no plan, really. First off he'd have to locate the men besieging the house. He flexed his strong fingers a moment and thought how pleasant it would be if he just had one by the throat right now. Guns had their place—of that there was no dispute—but real satisfaction came when a man could use just what God gave him. Shooting was far too good for gutless thieves taking advantage of war-born prejudices to rob honest folk. He'd barely got his saddle off the dun and was setting the picket pins when he heard a sound, like the click of a shod hoof against a rock. Silently he faded into the thick brush and waited, carbine in hand.

In the faint light the heads of two horses appeared over the rise, ears up and laid forward. Slowly they plodded on, heads bobbing and bit chains jingling in the time to a measured gait. They paused, and one whistled shrilly, bringing forth a snorting response from both of his own mounts, who shuffled their feet nervously and tossed their heads. Straining to make out the riders, he half lifted the carbine, a finger ready on the trigger. All he saw were two high-forked saddles, both empty. He shook his head and pawed at his eyes with the back of one hand. After the past two days without sleep, his vision was poor, and his brain felt numb.

Something hard prodded him in the small of his back. A hand grasped him by the shirt collar, and he was pushed into the clearing. "Aw right, mister, drop thet rifle, and be mighty quick doin' it! While you're about it, jest unbuckle thet gunbelt and let 'er fall." The voice had the sibilant softness of border Spanish, contrasting with the jargon he'd come to associate with West Texas cowboys.

"First off," he told the voice, "I'm not about to scratch up a nearly new Winchester by dropping it. Now, either you take it out of my hand or let me *lay* it down carefully. I have respect for my guns, and treat them accordingly."

"Huh? Listen, mister, them guns'll be worse'n scratched if you don't do like I said. You better shuck 'em now."

The two horses were very near, and behind them was a man

holding their tails in one hand. In his other was a short double-barreled shotgun pointed at McCowan's middle. Grinning, he gestured with the sawed-off. "I'd do like he was tellin' yuh, mister. Thet brother of mine is kinda edgy. I reckon he'd as soon kill yuh as not."

Grudgingly, McCowan laid down the rifle and loosened his gunbelt, his mind racing to gauge the situation. Carefully, he lowered the holstered pistol to rest on the carbine. Then he spoke, his voice slurred with weariness.

"Mind if I sit down?" he asked. "I've had no sleep for a couple of days, and I'm sorta tired. Besides, I been wanting a smoke, and I'd as leave do it sitting down." Neither of his grim-faced captors objected, so he squatted and took out his tobacco pouch and papers.

Picking up the Winchester and gunbelt, the second man led off the two horses and looped their reins over a tree limb at the edge of the clearing, while the other came around and stared at Trace suspiciously, a scowl on his dark face.

"Jest who are yuh, and what's your business?" he asked in that same soft tone. "This here's McCowan land, and you're durned lucky we didn't jest shoot you on sight."

Trace McCowan stared right back, his hands busy rolling a cigarette. Licking it, and giving that final twist, he patted his pockets for a match.

"I don't suppose you'd have a light?" he asked. "I'm fair parched for a smoke. Hard to roll one with a horse running flat out, and I didn't make many stops."

Automatically, the other reached into a shirt pocket and brought out a match, which he struck on the buttstock of his carbine. Leaning forward, he held it out in a cupped palm.

Like a striking snake, McCowan's hand flashed out, grasping the man's wrist in a viselike grip. With one powerful jerk he snatched the man off his feet and into his lap as with his right hand he reached back, whipping a long-bladed, razor-edged knife from the sheath between his shoulders. A moment later he held the man helpless, with the sharp blade against his throat.

"You! The brother to this one! If you value his life, I would suggest you lay down those guns, and carefully. That, of course, includes your own. Do it quick, now, or this man will die.'' Gently, he touched the knife edge to the skin in a slicing motion, and blood began to ooze along a thin line. Still holding the hapless man, he rose to his feet.

Bewildered, the other man hesitated for a moment, and the guttural sounds that spewed from his mouth in no way resembled the English language. Again he spoke, the hissing sibilance more like a turkey's gobble. The man McCowan held in his grasp was squirming and nodding his head. Whatever was being said was obviously a question, and there was no doubt, at least in McCowan's mind, as to what would be the answer.

Resignedly, the man laid down Trace's guns, together with the shotgun, and unbuckled his gunbelt, allowing it to slide to the ground. ''You got the drop on us now,'' he said bitterly. ''Jest you turn loose of my brother. Hurt him, and I swear I'll kill yuh with my bare hands.''

Trace already had his victim's revolver and carbine. His knife went back into its hiding place as he shoved the man toward his brother. ''Both of you get over by that saddle of mine,'' he instructed, ''and sit down with your hands held out in front of you. We're gonna have us a little talk.''

As they complied, he retrieved his own weapons and slung his gunbelt around his waist, drawing his revolver and making certain the caps were still in place. Slipping it back, he took a match from his vest pocket and fired up the cigarette he still held in his lips. Drawing in a mouthful, his face relaxed in a pleased smile, and he exhaled through both nostrils. ''Been looking forward to that,'' he told them.

Moving along the edge of the little clearing, he gathered up some twigs and several larger sticks. In moments, he'd put together a tiny fire, enough to give off some light, but not enough to be seen beyond the clearing. The first cigarette had only whetted his appetite for more, so he rolled another and lit it before sitting down with the Winchester in his lap.

''Now,'' he told them, ''let's have that little talk. What did you boys say your names were? You mentioned this as being McCowan land. Do you ride for the McCowans, or what?''

Neither man answered his questions. One dropped his gaze

toward the ground, and the other merely stared sullenly, a smoldering hate in his eyes. Trace could see something in them both that he'd failed to notice before. Not only were they obviously under twenty, but their features and darkness of skin labeled them as Indians. Or at least part-bloods, a trait they held in common with Abigail's boys. It was also an explanation of their unintelligible exchange of words.

"Supposing I start the ball rolling," McCowan told them, "by telling you my name's McCowan also. What would you say to that?"

The one he'd tricked was first to answer. "I'd say you were nothin' but a damn liar!" he burst out. "You look more like one of them Yankee sojers thet been tryin' to kill our cousins. Thet bunch thet's out there right now, shootin' a gun every time a McCowan shows his face at a winder."

"Nevertheless," Trace told them, "I am a McCowan, and I'd like you to believe that. Abigail is *my* cousin, since she's the daughter of my father's brother. I've almost killed two horses, riding day and night from Presidio, just so's I'd be able to help them out of this bind. Now tell me! Who are you two, and what are *you* doing out here?"

One looked at the other, and they both nodded. Jumping to his feet, the younger one held up his hand. "I am called Black Buffalo by my Kiowa people," he said. "But I'm really Pak McCowan, by adoption. This here's my brother, Tunk. He is Tunk-aht-oh-ye, the Thunderer, but like me, he's adopted into the McCowans. Do you have a plan? We've been out here for over a week but haven't helped a durn bit." He glanced over at his brother.

"Well, I take thet back. We did ketch us a couple out by their lone selves. Reckon they was tryin' to hunt up some fresh meat for the rest of their bunch. Show him, Tunk."

Pridefully, Tunk McCowan strutted over to where he'd tied their horses. Leading them over by the fire, he showed two fresh scalps woven into their manes. "Rush, he used to git real mad when we'd do somethin' like this," he told Trace.

"Yeah," his brother crowed. "But I doubt he'd pay it no mind now. Only thing I'm sorry about is us hidin' 'em out in the brush. We should've packed 'em over to where they've made their camp. Let 'em worry some, not knowin' who's next to git kilt. Mebbe they wouldn't be that cocky about takin' over the ranch. They'd be watchin' over their shoulders all the time, wonderin' what's behind every piece of brush.''

''Well,'' Trace told them, ''whatever we do, it's gonna have to wait until morning. I have to get some sleep. God! I'd sell my interest in hell for a drink right now. Don't suppose either one of you has a bottle? I thought not. Here's your guns back. Somebody'd best keep a guard's watch, in case a search party is out hunting the two you've done in. Me, I'm gonna roll up and get some shut-eye. Don't shake me unless a whiskey drummer happens by. Incidentally, you boys can call me Trace. That's my name—Trace McCowan.''

After stripping off the saddles and putting their horses on picket, the two boys sat and talked excitedly. Trace, a blanket pulled over him, went to sleep immediately. Typical of his race, Pak felt no anger toward the man who'd held a knife at his throat. Instead he took pride in the strength of this man who called himself Trace McCowan. Also in the fact that he'd been able to trick them and gain control. A trick that he would never forget, that just might come in handy.

In an old buffalo wallow half a mile away, a horse-sized mule watched disinterestedly as a big man in buckskins came over the rim and slid down the slope. Leaning his rifle on a blanket-draped saddle, the old-timer chuckled, half to himself and half to the mule. ''He, he, he! Thet boy purely ain't changed none. Yessir! Thet Trace is a chip off'n the old block, right enough. Slicked them two young'uns, and he never mussed a hair. Wouldn't do fer me to injun in on 'em—not tonight, anyways. Won't he be s'prised, seein' his pa! How long has it been? Nigh onto ten year, I reckon. Ain't seen me since he went back east, follerin' thet schoolmarm. Her with her fancy ways, and him taggin' along like a dog-wolf at breedin' time. Wonder how he come outta thet mess.''

Shrugging out of the pouch and unbuckling his gunbelt, a thought struck him as he laid them aside and made ready to sleep. S'posin' he ain't forgivin'? Mebbe he ain't never forgot how I stole his share of the fur money. I only done it so's he'd have to stay and trap. It warn't the gold I'd wanted. I jest didn't want him makin' a fool of hisself. A groan escaped him as he lay down by the saddle. Seemed as how the ground got harder as he grew older.

He'd already been to reconnoiter the enemy camp, and he knew that by himself he could do little beyond picking off a few of them from a distance. Getting through their lines so as to join those in the house would be absurdly easy, but that would serve no purpose. It had been a real lucky stroke that he had stumbled on the two boys. Curious, he had followed them into the clearing; watched as they put their heads together, made their plan, and went after his son. He chuckled. It might have worked out fine if their victim had been anyone but a McCowan. McCowans got their training early on, and to give in just wasn't their notion, no matter what the odds.

Reaching up with a gnarled fist, he tugged off a wolfskin cap and raised his eyes to the stars overhead. "Lord, we might jest be needful of Your help t'morrow. If it pleases You, look kindly on this pore old sinner who's standin' in the sight of all Thy bounty, Lord. Purely, the right is all on our side, 'cause Abigail and her sons be decent folk. I ask thet these old eyes hold true to the target and strike down them evildoers like a scythe cuts prairie hay. Amen."

A faint light showed in the east when the old man rolled out of his blanket. He wasted little time in breaking camp. The mule, wise to his ways, didn't bother to resist the saddle, or the bit thrust between his teeth. In minutes every sign of their presence had been erased: even the tracks left by the mule were smoothed over by a mesquite branch that was trailed behind as they climbed out of the wallow.

Wouldn't do to pussyfoot around, the oldster decided. He would just ride on in and take his medicine. Perhaps circumstance was on his side. The boy . . . Boy? Hell! Trace'd never see forty again. Boy, he was not. Anyways, maybe the fact that they were all there for the same purpose might be in his favor. Squaring his shoulders, he nudged the mule.

Twenty minutes later he was staring into the muzzle of a rifle, and the man holding it wore the uniform of a soldier. Behind him were three more, all in Yankee blue, with smiles on their faces. One in the rear held reins to four horses.

"Well! Just what d'we have here?" one remarked. "What's *your* name, old man? Daniel Boone?" He guffawed, and so did his companions. "Here we are," said the man with the rifle, "out looking for fresh meat, and we caught ourselves a real live old bull. Looking at him, I'd say the meat'd be tough. Too tough to be very tasty." He stopped smiling.

"Who are you, and what are you doing out here this early in the day? You're too old to have been a Johnny Reb, and I doubt you're scouting for our side. C'mon, speak up! Don't be just staring like you'd—"

"Hell, Sergeant," one of the others said with a grin. "I don't see why you're wasting time with the old geezer. What do you say? Let's just shoot the old buzzard and have done with him. Anyways, I've always wanted me one of them fringed buckskin shirts. His looks like it ain't been too near a bar of soap, but I can fix that. Go ahead. Careful, so's you don't put no bullet holes in my new shirt."

A bullet passed so close to the old man that he felt the wind of its passage, and a blue hole suddenly appeared just above the sergeant's right eye. His head jerked back, and a groan, partially muffled by the sound of the shot, came from his lips as his body slumped to the ground.

The mule reared, and the oldster's revolver bucked in his fist as he shot one of the others in the chest. More shots were heard, and then he was staring dazedly at the motionless bodies of all four men and listening to the retreating sounds of their terrified horses. Two riders charged out of the brush and swept past him, close on the heels of the animals, as he struggled to bring the mule under control.

"Hey! You okay, old-timer?" Trace McCowan materialized out of the thick cover, a look of concern on his face. Then his eyes widened and he took a step back. "Pop? Is that really you, Pop? I sure never expected to—"

"You're durn tootin' it's me," the oldster replied testily. "Who'd you think it was? Moses lookin' fer a burnin' bush or sump'n? Well! Don't jest stand there, durn ye! I ain't no ghost. You can at least take my hand." He climbed down from the mule, who was beginning to act as if he'd much rather be somewhere else, away from the sound of gunfire and the smell of freshly spilled blood.

Warily they each extended a hand, circling, neither willing to make the first move toward restoring the father-son relationship. Then Trace took a step forward and threw both his arms around the old man. "You old devil," he said huskily, a tear showing in each eye. "I've really missed you!"

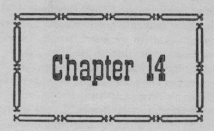

Chapter 14

I tell ye, it's unnatchul!'' Justice McCowan twisted in his saddle and plucked in distaste at the undersized blue uniform he was wearing. ''Thet feller'll come back to ha'nt me fer rollin' him under a bush with nothin' but his long drawers. 'Sides, this here outfit has blood all over it.''

Trace smiled patiently. ''It won't be for very long; I promise you that, Pop. It's the only way we're gonna get in reasonably close to that outfit without drawing fire. Come up with a better idea and I'll surely go along with it.''

The old man scowled, but he knew his son was right. He squinted back at the two Indian boys, who were also wearing uniforms that they'd taken from the four dead men. Up ahead, almost two miles distant, was the main camp of the invaders.

"I still figger it'd be better to wait fer dark," he told his son. "Them fellers'd have to be idjits not to rec'nize the four of us as bein' strangers."

"That doesn't figure into it," Trace explained. "We'll begin firing as soon as we're within range. Knock down all we can, and then ride hell-bent for the ranch house. Should be easy enough to do, because we'll have the advantage of complete surprise. By the time they realize what's going on, we'll have done our work and gotten out of there. They won't know what hit them. Believe me, Pop, this'll work."

"Lucky we ketched up their horses," Tunk called out. "If they'd showed up in thet camp, we wouldn't have *no* chance."

Trace nodded. "Right enough," he agreed. They rode on in silence, each with his own thoughts about what lay ahead. In spite of his assurance, Trace knew the chance they'd be taking. Once through the camp, they'd still have the mile-long ride to the ranch house. He chuckled. Plainly, somebody in the house, probably Milo, had convinced those in the camp of the long-range potential of a Sharps rifle; even at a mile, they weren't completely safe from a killing shot, had Milo wanted to experiment with sight settings.

"Remember," Trace called out. "Use the short guns first off, and save the rifle loads for later." They'd each taken the Army Colts from the four dead men, and so had a gun for each hand. All their belt guns now held six rounds, since he had advised them to load the chamber normally left empty.

"Another thing." Trace glanced over at the two boys. "We *are* wearing these uniforms, so there ain't no way the people in the house can know we're their friends. You two had best stay out in front as we head for the house. They'll recognize you, but they might just shoot holes in me 'n' Pop. Toss away those Army hats so's they can see your faces, and holler loud when you get in close enough for them to hear. It would be a shame to get shot by our own folks after pulling off a neat trick like this."

Justice McCowan was still grumbling. Riding behind the

others so his mule wouldn't be seen by those in the camp, a dust cloud to the east caught his eye.

"You still got them glasses you taken off the sergeant?" he asked his son. "Lemme borry 'em fer jest a minute." He peered through them, twirling the knurled wheel to bring in a clearer focus. Then he let out a tremendous whoop.

"*Woooo hah!* We got us company, and they're friendly. I swan! It's my brother-in-law, Handsome Horse. Him and the whole durn Choctaw Nation, look's like. Well . . . at least mebbe twenty of 'em. What d'we do now? By damn! If we was jest a mite closer, so's we could let him know who we are . . . This way, he'll figger us fer jest some more durn soldiers and shoot at us afore we can tell him otherwise."

"Too late to change our plan," Trace told him. "We'll go in just like we figured. Once we start shooting, maybe the Indians will understand that we're on their side. We still better head for the house once our guns are shot empty. If we just play out our hand, I believe it'll turn out fine."

Fifteen minutes later, with a half mile yet to go, it was apparent that they'd lost the element of surprise. Although their own presence was taken for granted, sentries had spotted the Indians' column, and preparations were being made to defend the camp. A bugle sounded, and men were pouring from the tents, grabbing at stacked rifles, and running toward a perimeter on the outer edge.

Pak shouted something at Trace, and both he and Tunk were pointing excitedly at a knot of men on the nearest side of the encampment. The men were tugging at what looked to be a length of pipe mounted on a set of wheels. Another man was running toward them leading a harnessed team of horses.

"What's thet?" he hollered. "Some sorta cannon, or what? Looks like they're mebbe gonna move it."

Shading his eyes against the early morning sun, Trace had a moment of sudden fear. "Hell, no!" he shouted back, his spine tingling with apprehension. "That's a Gatling, and we got us a real problem. One gun like that one has the same firepower as a hundred riflemen and can mean the difference between winning and losing battles. In our case, whether or not we'll be watching the sun come up tomorrow or buzzards coming in to pick our bones. We gotta do something, and the sooner the better." He paused and stared at the two boys.

"Which one of you is the better roper?" he asked. "I mean really good. Able to put your rope on target no matter how tough that target might be. Hurry now, because we haven't a lot of time. Who's the best all-around roper?"

The boys stared at him for a moment, then turned back to watch the soldiers straining with the heavy gun. "Well, I reckon it's more like a toss-up," Pak told him laconically. "Seems like when one of us gits real good at sump'n, then the other goes him one better. Been like thet since we was jest li'l fellers. What've you got in mind to do?"

"We're gonna take the gun away from them," Trace informed him. "We're gonna ride in there, rope that gun, and drag it as far away as we can. Enough so that the Indians can get in safely and do what has to be done. Are you game to try it, boys? If not, just say so, and we'll figure out another way to go." He looked away. "I'll understand," he added.

"No reason why we can't both dab a rope on it, is there?" Tunk had already taken his riata in his hands and built his loop—a small one, no bigger than he used to catch up mounts in the horse corral. "I'm ready," he told Trace. "I figger we're jest wastin' time here. Let's git the job done."

Trace nodded and looked back at his father. "All set, Pop?" he asked, a grin softening his craggy features.

The big man smiled back and lifted his Colts, the mule's reins wound around one blue-clad arm. "You jest call out a tune, son. Me 'n' old Lucifer here is all ready to sashay."

"Well then," Trace told him, "this here's how I figure to do it. You boys give us your extra Colts, 'cause you have plenty to do just with handling that Gatling. Me 'n' Pop are gonna cover you as best we can. We'll concentrate on those armed men close by, and drop as many as we can. Don't waste time worrying about them shooting back, because they'll fire at us to protect themselves. Just rope that gun and ride. If you can get even a hundred yards away before they understand what we're trying to do, then I think you'll be safe." He paused and looked them over. "Remember, a hundred yards away," he repeated. "Beyond that, their chances of making an accurate shot are few and far between. Don't look back, and don't worry about us. We'll be right behind you."

Emulating his father, he looped his reins around one arm and cocked both Colts. "Let's go," he told them, spurring the big bay into a hard run.

Soundlessly, they bore down on the gun crew, the hoofs of their mounts muffled by the thick prairie sod. As they drew within range, the four riders formed abreast and swept down on the camp, Trace and the old man firing with both hands.

With hoarse cries the soldiers abandoned the Gatling as bullets began to find their marks. His long hair streaming, Justice let go a spine-tingling whoop as he cocked and fired the Colts, each shot dropping a man in his tracks. Some, writhing on the ground, called out for help, but most stayed where they'd fallen. Caught off guard by the sudden attack, the demoralized men were unable to put up much of a defense. Most were armed with muzzle-loading rifles, which were slow and hard to reload properly in a panic situation, and much too cumbersome for this type of close-in fighting. A few had picketed their own horses nearby and were able to get mounted, which only added to the general confusion.

Dust rose in choking clouds, stirred by the plunging feet of the horses, making it even more difficult to tell friend from attacking foe. To the soldiers it appeared that these mounted demons were everywhere and numbered in the dozens.

One with yellow corporal's chevrons on his sleeves was apparently a veteran of battles like this and knelt down to take careful aim at the rampaging old mountain man. Before he could touch off the round, a bullet from Trace's left-hand gun tore through his throat. Dropping his unfired rifle, he managed a strangled squawk before falling over on his side.

The hammer of Trace's right-hand Colt snapped on an empty as he swung to face a man on foot no more than ten yards away. Caught in the act of reloading, the man brought up a Springfield rifle with a ramrod protruding from the muzzle. His face contorted in fear and anger, the soldier yanked the trigger in panic,

sending the rod whistling by Trace's head; it narrowly missed
him as he ducked behind his horse's neck.

Openmouthed, the man stood for an instant, staring, with the
empty rifle in his hands. Trace had jammed the revolver in his
holster and slid another from his belt. Cocking the gun, he
aimed it at the unfortunate's heaving chest.

"Aw, hell," he muttered. "There'll be another time." A
look of disgust crossed his face, and he waved the barrel of the
gun in the man's direction. "If you figured on living a whole lot
longer," he said, "then I'd suggest you get on out of here.
You'd best show me your heels, mister, 'cause if I see you
standing there after I count to three, then you're a dead man.
One . . . two . . . and . . ." The man threw down the rifle
and ran, heading across the open prairie as if hounds were
snapping at his heels. Looking around, Trace surveyed the field
of battle with some satisfaction.

The abandoned Gatling had tilted, with the trail pointing high
in the air and the muzzle buried in the ground. Quick to take the
advantage, both the boys made perfect casts, the loops drawing
tight around the uplifted trail. Their short, Texas-style ropes
were already tied fast to the horns, and a moment later Trace
exulted as they rode from the camp, the Gatling in tow and
bounding along in their wake.

They'd made short work of the gun crew, but Trace and his
father could see men running from the distant perimeter. "I
reckon we'd best be on our way," Trace shouted. "We've
done all we came to do. Let's get the heck out of here!"

With one Colt back in its holster and the other thrust in his
belt, Justice was standing tall in his stirrups, paying little mind
to bullets hitting around him. One, droning by his ear, came so
close he felt its heat. Another tugged at his shirt, and a third
whined off a nearby rock. Lifting the old caplock rifle, heedless
of the near misses, he took careful aim and squeezed the trigger
ever so gently. Flame belched from the rifle's muzzle, and a
sharp crack echoed across the campground. One of those in the
lead stumbled as a shriek came from his lips, and he fell head-
long.

"D'yuh see thet?" the old man cried. "Nailed him betwixt

the horns, jest as purty as you please! I . . .'' He reeled in the saddle, then slumped forward over the pommel, his hands clutching at the horn.

Trace had heard the sodden thump as the bullet hit home, and knew its meaning. Socking his spurs to the bay, he was by his father's side in an instant and grabbing at his arm. ''Hold on, Pop!'' he hollered. ''I'll have you out of here in no time at all. Just hold on. For God's sake, hold on!''

His great hand opened long enough to add his father's reins to his own. With his other brawny arm wrapped around the old man's shoulders, he wheeled both mounts and savagely spurred them into a lumbering run. He could feel wetness soaking through the woolen shirt, and knew that his father's wound was a bad one, and perhaps fatal.

Ahead of him he could see the two boys with the Gatling gun rolling behind. Both had discarded the Army hats, along with the shirts, and were whooping and hollering to those in the ranch house. Trace could hear the wind-whipped howls of triumph, and he prayed they would be understood.

''Don't shoot, Milo! Ain't nobody but us! We brung you a present, and it's a real dandy! Open up, Milo. We're comin' in, and sorta in a hurry!''

Fighting to keep his father's limp form in the saddle as their mounts slammed together and surged apart, Trace's arm was nearly jerked out of its socket, and his leg, caught in between, was wrenched and bruised from the impact. Wincing, he tightened his grip and spurred the bay horse.

''We're almost there,'' he gritted through clenched teeth. ''Not much further, Pop! Hang on and we'll make it, you and me. You can't die on me! Not now! Not after all we've been through!'' He peered from under his hat brim. Not more than a couple of hundred yards and they'd be safe at the house.

Behind him he could hear shouting and the sounds of gunfire. If any of the bullets came close, he wasn't able to feel them pass. More shots now, but these were coming from in front of him. Oh, God, he groaned to himself. If they don't know who we are, we're dead meat. He roweled the bay again, and they

raced even faster, but he could feel an unevenness to the animal's stride and felt him falter.

The mule, seeming to sense what was required of him, kept
trying to maintain an interval, but Trace's bay wanted nothing
to do with the long-eared animal and tried constantly to edge
away. Cursing, Trace yanked at the horse's head in an effort to
bring him into line. Finally, with only twenty yards left to go,
he balled his fist and struck the horse a tremendous blow between the ears.

The animal's legs spraddled out, and he fell, dragging his
rider out of the saddle, still clinging to the old man. For an instant Trace hung on, but the mule's hoofs were hitting his boots
and threatened to run him over. He let go, and a moment later
his legs went out from under him and he rolled in the dirt of the
ranch yard, the mule's hind feet barely missing his head. Shad-
owy figures were reaching for him, and he struck out at them in
fear and bewilderment. My pop is dying, he screamed, but the
words were trapped inside his head and wouldn't come out.
Dazedly, he felt himself lifted, and then blackness came. . . .

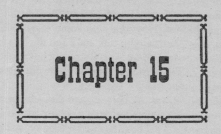

Chapter 15

I'd sat Carlos next to a window so he could keep his eye out for guards while we talked with Mr. Gilkie. Strange, I reckon, but I'd always called him that, even though he was a colored man, and hired help to boot. 'Course, he *was* older, and Ma'd always taught us boys to respect our elders, but I believe it was more than just his age. He had a way of putting things that made you realize his worth. He had him an education of sorts, and he'd read every book in the ranch's well-stocked library. Even more'n book knowledge, he had an ability to do most anything, and do it well. Anyway, he was my good friend, and I thought an awful lot of him.

It was coming onto eight o'clock, and we'd have to hurry our planning. The captain had said we'd eat about eight, so somebody could come anytime now. Mr. Gilkie had knocked at the panel right after sundown, and we'd been talking since then. He'd counted about five hundred cartridges stored in the hidden room, but only three rifles to fire them. He had a shotgun, he told me, with about twenty loads, and his own personal handgun, a French LeMat. Now that was some gun, I want to tell you. A revolver, it had two barrels and fired ten shots. The inventor, Dr. Alexandre LeMat, was living in New Orleans when war broke out. A Southern sympathizer, he went back to Paris in '61 and made the guns for the South.

The regular barrel was .42 caliber, and the cylinder held nine shots. The cylinder revolved around another, five-inch barrel set below that was .63 caliber and fired buckshot. A man carrying that gun was almost like a whole army by his lone self and could sure do some damage. Loaded, it weighed about four pounds, so he carried it suspended from a leather sling rather than in a belt holster.

Not having a small gun that I could hide under my shirt, he'd offered me a long double-edged knife. One I could put in my boot. I'd thanked him but turned down the offer. No way I could explain it, but I'd never much cared for cutting a man up with a knife. Much rather use my hands on him.

Lancelot Gilkie was a medium-sized man, and not strongly built, but I'd seen him pitch vaqueros to the ground more'n twice his size. It was some trick that he'd learned from a Chinaman, or so he'd told me, and it worked every time. Nobody tried to mess with him, at least not more'n once.

Once we'd got done with the howdies and the handshakes, I figgered it was time we did some planning. Mr. Gilkie had a plan of sorts, but like he told us, it was a long way from being foolproof. There were too many ifs to consider.

"You can forget about the thirty-four vaqueros locked in the bunkhouses," he told us. "Them Yankees guard 'em close, day 'n' night, and a *cucaracha* couldn't crawl in or out. Why, I tried to sneak in close enough so I could tell 'em what's been goin' on, and I danged near got ketched. Them soldiers *know* what could happen to 'em if your vaqueros had a chance to lay their hands on them, and they ain't about to let even one git away. Them riders remember what was done to Aragon, and they're plenty mad, but ain't no chance to spring 'em.

"Howsomever," he went on, "their women ain't under guard, and some can come and go jest as they please. I heard many were bothered at first, but the captain raised Cain. Posted an order promising a whipping for any man who molested a woman. Bein' free to move around, they could sure help us."

Don Carlos looked at him in amazement. "Surely you'd not consider using a *woman* to fight these soldiers? I could never permit it. Bad enough to have the deaths of my men on my conscience without subjecting defenseless women to pain, and possibly even death. I cannot allow this."

Mr. Gilkie wasn't about to give in. "Look, *patrón,* the Indian women fight alongside of their men if necessary. The fact is, women can be more cruel and heartless than any man might possibly be. Ask anyone who has ever seen a prisoner tortured by Indians. It's always the women who think up all the really terrible things thet're done to prisoners."

He held up his hand. "Please, *patrón.* Give me time to finish what I have to say. I have talked with these women. B'lieve me, they are ready. Ready to do most anything that will give them back their men and make things normal.

"Now," he went on, "here's what I got in mind. Some of the women agreed to do maid service for the officers and to wash clothes and such for the whole bunch. Nobody's doin' this out of the goodness of their hearts. Thet captain told 'em their men would suffer if they didn't cooperate. Thet there's the word he used, I b'lieve, *cooperate,* and he meant it.

"In a way, that helps us, 'cause the women can come 'n' go without bein' questioned. They can go into the kitchen and grab a knife or two. There's even a chance that they'd find firearms in an officer's room, but we won't count on it. A lot of ranch tools can be used as weapons—machetes, sickles, and hoes. They're all mighty sharp and can cut a man purty bad. Every man outta action means we can use his guns, and once we got enough of 'em, we'll free the vaqueros and take back this here rancho."

Carlos looked sick. "I don't know. If any of the women were hurt, I could never forgive myself. I couldn't stand the sight of them lying wounded, or worse. A woman is a precious creature and must be protected."

"Thet's another thing," Gilkie announced. "I'm certain we'd all feel easier if you weren't around when we start in fightin' the soldiers, so part of the plan is to sneak you 'n' Miss Esperanza away from the rancho before anything happens here. Thet way, we can—"

"No!" Carlos almost shouted the word. "This is *my* home, and I will not leave its defense to others. I may not be a whole man physically, but I can still handle a rifle. I'll not run away when danger threatens. Noth . . ." He paused.

"You're probably right," he said wearily. "Having me to worry about would only add to your problem. *A sus ordenes,* old friend. I am willing to do as you have suggested."

"Thank you, *patrón.* Believe me, we will be very careful, and I will not risk anybody's life, includin' my own." With a smile, Mr. Gilkie reached out and taken Carlos's hand.

"Here they come," Carlos hissed. "Four of them, and no time to waste. You must go, my friend, and quickly. Hurry, Lysander, help him close the panel behind him. They are very close, and will be here at any moment."

The same two guards came to fetch us to supper, and they brought along two others, with a funny-looking chair. Wooden shafts stuck out in front and back, and straps of leather hung in loops from the ends. I'd barely got the panel back in place before they were banging on the door, after first rattling the knob and finding the door locked.

I made sure nothing was out of place, and dusted over the panel with my neckerchief before I walked over and unlocked the heavy door. The chubby guard seemed to be in charge, and he pushed past me, peering suspiciously around the room. After a moment he motioned to the others, and they came in carrying the specially rigged chair.

The fat one asked Carlos to sit in the chair, and I helped to lift him in. My arm was feeling much stronger, but no reason for them knowing, I figgered. So I made a big show and groaned some when I taken hold.

The fat guard smirked. "Hurts, doesn't it, big fellow? Too bad the captain didn't cut that arm clean off, after the way you treated Mr. Gresham. Consider yourself very lucky."

I stared down at him, and my hands twitched to get a hold of his fat neck and twist his thick head off his shoulders. He must have seen the malevolence in my eyes, and read it as such, because he quick-like moved in behind one of the other guards, his face reddened, and his breathing got heavy.

"You make one false move, you big ox," he said shrilly, "and we'll fill you so full of holes you won't hold water. Just 'cause they're keeping you alive don't mean they'd miss you that much. You'll see! You'll see! Now! You stand hitched over there, and don't you dare move till I tell you so. I'd as soon kill you as look at your ugly face."

His last insult had really hit home, but I couldn't let a poor excuse for a man like him know it had bothered me. I reached up and fingered the thick scab that had formed over the wound. "Ugly" was right! How could any woman keep on caring when her man had the scarred, twisted look of a monster? Esperanza had said she loved me, but that was now. A year from now, would she still feel the same? Could anyone, much less a beautiful woman, go through her lifetime living with such ugliness? Was it fair for me to ask it of her? I reckon some of the thoughts showed in my expression, because a knowing grin was on the fat man's face, and he chuckled.

"Ah, ha! I hit a sore spot, didn't I, you big moose! It sure is a shame, ain't it? Young as you are, and with a lot of pretty muscles for the women to admire, you'd have to put a feed sack over your head when you went calling. Ain't no woman gonna stand the sight of you, much less want you holding her hand. But don't you worry none, bucko, 'cause your courting days just might be over. Ha, ha, ha! Lookit that, boys! Ain't he about the ugliest critter you ever did see? Wait! You hold on there! You hold on or I'll shoot!"

I had taken a step in his direction, and he backed up in terror and jerked a gun from his belt. Trembling, he aimed it at my belly, and I saw his knuckles whiten as his finger tightened on the trigger. The sweat had popped out on his forehead, and he was swaying like he might collapse.

The guard nearest him reached out and grabbed the barrel of the gun, pushing it away. "Leggo of the gun, Bert," he ordered, "or you'll have us all in trouble. You know how we stand with the captain already. One more dumb trick like this and he'll have us in front of a firing squad, or worse than that—maybe a hangman's rope. You can't blame this man for getting riled. Now lay off him and put that damn gun away. And you"—he pointed at me—"you just keep that temper of yours under control, you hear? You sure ain't in no position to risk losing it, because it might just get you killed. You think about that.

"Now!" He turned to the others. "Bert's gonna lead us on in and handle one set of shafts. Frank, you grab a hold on the other and we'll be on our way. I want no more talk and no more foolishness. Is that understood?"

The fat man started to say something, then thought better of it. He thrust the gun back in his belt and helped raise the chair. The one who had wrested the gun away got in back of me, along with the remaining guard, and we headed for the dining room. I glanced at Carlos and saw one eye close in a gleeful wink. He was sure a cheerful cuss, and I couldn't figger out why, under the circumstances.

The table in the ranch dining room was a long one, and it seated about twenty. The stout middle-aged man was sitting at one end when we came into the room. He rose and made a big show of mock geniality, lifting his glass and asking an officer to usher us to our seats. Carlos, of course, needed only a place to park, so the young lieutenant put him at the opposite end of the table, where he faced our smiling host.

Still standing, the stocky civilian spoke to me. "Your name, sir, must be Lysander McCowan. I am Silas P. Gresham, the federal land commissioner for western Texas. Next to me is my chief aide, Lucius M. Dills, recently lieutenant colonel, U.S.

Army, now honorably retired after many years of service to this wonderful country of ours.''

I stared. The man next to him had been talking to some feller in civilian clothes, but now he turned around with a sour grin on his face. It was that Dills feller, all right, the one I'd shot through the shoulder back in Sycamore Canyon. His left arm was in a sling, and there was no humor in his smile.

''We've met,'' I told Gresham, and said no more. Dills had already turned around and resumed his conversation with the other man, apparently not wanting to be bothered.

I saw no sign of the captain, and that had me worried. A sheathed saber was hanging from the back of a chair next to Gresham, and I figgered that was the captain's sword, but no sign of him or Esperanza was to be seen.

''Well, Mr. McCowan, I must say the circumstances are not exactly the same as when we first met, are they?'' Gresham, still smiling, strolled around the table and stopped just a few feet from my chair. ''As I recall, you seemed somewhat over-wrought at the time. Something about a filthy, disfigured half savage that my men were forced to shoot. You saw fit to hold me to blame, it seemed, and threw me across this very room. Lucky for me, and for you also, I wasn't hurt.''

Hang on, I told myself. Don't let him rile you. Not a thing you can do about it, leastways, not just now. Forgive me, Poco Luce. I ain't forgot, and you can believe that. I promise I'll get revenge. This here grinning snake'll wish he'd never laid eyes on us before I'm done with him. It'll mebbe take a bit more time, but I'll get him good.

To try and mask my feelings wasn't easy, but I managed to do so. I nodded to him as I reached into a pocket, fishing out my tobacco pouch. ''You mind?'' I asked, holding up pouch and papers. He shook his head, so I proceeded to build me a cigarette and light it while he stared at me curiously.

He emptied his glass and crooked his finger at a soldier nearby who was wearing an apron over his uniform. ''Bring the wine over here, if you please, Corporal. Would you care for an-other, Mr. McCowan? It's an excellent wine, made here on the premises, or so I've been given to understand. Every bit as good as those French or Italian vintages. It's been my contention that we make a mistake in regarding the local products as inferior to those from abroad. Really not logical, you know, and certainly not patriotic. Looking at them from an economic standpoint, we'd do well to utilize our own manufacture. Don't you agree, young man?''

Wellsir, I didn't know what to think, and much less what to say. Either this man was completely loony or I'd forgot what made sense anymore. Here we were, being held prisoner in Carlos's house while this madman spouted a lot of crazy, nonsensical talk about wine. A stranger would have figgered the house was Gresham's and we were just some neighbors he had invited over to a shindig. He was polite as pie, and as gracious as any host could be. What was he leading up to? I wondered. What did he stand to gain by all his courtesy and fine manners? And why did he feel it was necessary?

My thoughts were interrupted by a flurry of movements by the door. Turning my head, I saw Esperanza. She wore the same black gown I remembered from last year's *baile*. Quite a party, that had been. It was the first time I'd ever seen her, and I'd fallen in love on the spot.

A tortoiseshell comb sparkling with small diamonds was high on the back of her head, and a lacy black mantilla lay close to her cheeks. She was far lovelier than any woman I had ever seen, and she lit up the room like a million lamps, or ten times that many candles.

Marring her entrance was the skinny captain, who wore the blue dress uniform he'd worn more'n a week before, on that day he'd slashed me with his saber. His left arm was held a bit crooked, and Esperanza's hand was flat on his sleeve as they entered. His expression was smug as he bowed and acknowledged greetings from the other officers.

Dills and his civilian friend were right in there, and I could see the ex-colonel was none too happy about how things had been arranged. He leaned forward and said something to the captain and got a vigorous headshake for an answer. It was obvious to me that he'd mebbe suggested that the lady'd be happier with him as an escort but had been turned down.

Gresham seemed to be in no hurry to greet them, and I had to wonder why. Then I understood. He'd left my side to return to his chair at the head of the table. The corporal was pouring him another glass of wine, and he lolled back in the thronelike chair, waiting for them to come to him.

The last time I'd seen that chair was the day I'd got me this scar. Further back, I remembered Carlos sitting there when the dying grulla had wandered in, packing what was left of poor Aragon lashed to its back with rawhide. Now this little pipsqueak of a man dared to take on airs, like he was the master and the rest of us'd better sit up and listen. It galled me. To think that this puffed-up frog of a man could sit there in Don Carlos's chair and treat us like the dirt under his feet! I gripped the arms of my chair and forced myself to calm down. To go off half-cocked again would be downright foolishness. Why, this plump ape wouldn't make a pimple on a sheepherder's rear end. My chance would come.

The captain had escorted Esperanza to where Gresham waited, and made a big show of bowing and making introductions. I saw Gresham reach out and snag her hand, then kiss it on the back before she pulled it away. I chuckled when I saw her wipe it off across the back of her dress. From the expression on her face, you'd swear she'd accidentally stuck the hand in something nasty.

Apparently he didn't see it done, because he was wearing a big smile as he gestured them to chairs on his right. He insisted that Esperanza sit next to him, although an unhappy captain was holding back the other chair for her. Motioning to the corporal, who was hovering close by, Gresham asked him to fill their glasses.

From the puzzled look on Esperanza's face, I guessed he was spouting some more of that gibberish about wines, and why we should stock our own. She looked across at me, a half smile on her lips and her eyebrows raised. I shrugged my shoulders and grinned as Gresham kept on jabbering away at her, seemingly unaware of our exchange.

A heavyset soldier wearing a tall white chef's hat of some sort came up to Gresham and bent down. He said something to him, then straightened up and hurried away. Picking up a spoon, Gresham tinkled it against his wineglass so as to get everybody's attention.

"Our dinner is about to be served," he said, "so I'd very much appreciate everyone taking their seats. Colonel Dills, if you would be so kind, and bring your friend with you. We shall begin in just a moment."

A procession of soldiers came from the kitchen and began serving the meal. A huge beef roast was placed in front of Gresham and he began to carve, calling out our names, so he would know just how we wanted our portions. It was all like a bad dream, one of those nightmares where you know that you are dreaming, that none of this is really happening, and that at any moment you will wake up.

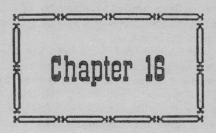

Chapter 16

After we'd eaten, more soldiers came in and cleared away the dishes. Two good-sized pots of coffee were put down on one end of the table, the one nearest Carlos, and brandy and cigars were placed nearby, convenient to our reach.

Gresham had sent most of his guests from the room, except for Carlos, Esperanza, and me. Dills remained behind, as did the captain, and two burly sergeants wearing sidearms stationed themselves near the closed door.

The six of us were sitting fairly close together. "So we can speak without having to raise our voices," Gresham told us. "No reason to let everyone know our business," he said.

Loosening his tie, he selected a cigar from the box, took a

small knife from his vest pocket, and carefully trimmed an end. Peering at us from under heavy brows, he asked why we seemed so glum.

"After all," he said, "you've just put away an excellent dinner, one prepared by the greatest chef the U.S. Army has ever trained. You've been treated courteously, as my honored guests, and I have spared nothing in making you feel like this might be your own home."

If Carlos could have leaped to his feet about then, I do believe he would have done so. His face turned even darker, and the veins stood out on his neck like ropes as he struggled to speak. "Señor," he said, "you forget. This *is* my home. My revered ancestor, Pedro Rozadura y Golondrina, was a soldier in the armies of Spain and received this grant of land from his king. When your grandfather's grandfather was safe in Europe, mine was completing thirty years of service in the New World. He fought to win this land, and he fought to keep it, as did my father, who was gravely wounded while serving with Colonel Fannin at Goliad. This grant was confirmed by the Republic of Texas, and again confirmed by the state. By what right can you treat it as yours?"

He paused and took a deep breath. "What you have done here is unbelievable. It's the act of a pirate, or perhaps the word 'madman' is more descriptive, since by your insane, maundering words, you lead one to believe you've taken leave of your senses.

"You came in here under false pretenses and then declared me a traitor and my property as forfeit. Yet not once have you shown me documents that might show your actions as being legal ones. To add to this," he continued, "you speak of us as though we are your guests when in reality we are your prisoners. You've caused the deaths of many of my men, and locked up the others, although they have done nothing to you. Now tell me, what is it you want from me? What must be done to bring things back to normal? What can *I* do now that you have taken this drastic step, one from which you've no retreat? Surely you must realize that those truly having authority will not let you go unpunished. How can I insure the safety of my daughter, my friends, and my vaqueros? To confiscate this ranch is one thing; to take it over, using force of arms and killing us all, is quite another. The continuation of this farce, with the playacting and all of these maudlin, idiotic fantasies, is beyond belief. Surely you must be aware of this. You can't get away with it. You can't kill over seventy persons and not have someone know.''

Gresham took his cigar from his mouth and sighed. ''If you are deliberately trying to make me angry,'' he said, ''beware of what you say, because you might succeed. I hold the power of life or death over every one of you. This 'farce,' as you term it, is a deadly serious game, and you, or any of these others, could simply disappear if I gave the order. If you doubt this, reflect on what you have already seen and experienced. My men and I are in complete control.

''Have you perhaps wondered,'' he went on, ''why nobody made an effort to rescue you? Why not one single rancher showed up here asking for you and wanting to know what an army is doing at Rancho Montoncillo? Why McCowan's brother isn't at the front gate, threatening to batter it down? Well, señor, there's a very good reason. You may be certain of that.'' He smiled. ''I shall allow the colonel to give you answers to these questions. I am tiring of you.''

Dills frowned and adjusted the sling on his arm. ''The Mc-Cowan ranch is undoubtedly ours at this very moment. One of our cavalry troops surrounded the house early this week, with orders to kill anyone who resisted. The deputy marshal for this district accompanied them, with complete authority and permission to use force. The troop included a trained and experienced crew, with a Gatling rapid-fire gun. At any moment I expect to receive a messenger with the results of this expedition and a casualty count.''

My heart was turning flip-flops about then, but I wasn't all that scared. Milo had lots of experience with this sort of thing, and gosh knows he had a fine arsenal. We'd built the house like a regular fort, and it would take more than a Gatling gun to breach those walls. Nevertheless, I didn't like the thought of my family in danger, and some of my concern must have shown in my expression. The colonel smirked, satisfied that he had gotten through to me, and continued.

"At the same time, runners were sent to all the neighboring ranches, notifying the owners of your arrest for the crime of conspiracy. You'll get no help from them, since we included details of your intentions to take over all of West Texas and force them from their homes. From what I've been given to understand, there was talk of hanging you, and some volunteered to hoist the ropes." He sat down with a smile.

Gresham raised his glass to his lips and peered over the rim. "In spite of what you might think of me, I am a fair man. My men and I have discussed this thoroughly and feel that you should be compensated in some way, so . . . I have a fair offer for you. In return for signing a quit-claim deed to this ranch property, I will advance you sufficient money so that you may leave the state of Texas, taking any of your employees who do not wish to work for me.

"Naturally, we will not allow you any weapons. You might be foolish and attempt to attack the ranch and wrest it away from us. However, believe me! As of this moment, Texas doesn't want you as citizens. Your former friends would not hesitate to hang you to the nearest tree if you insisted on staying. We have done our job thoroughly, and there is not one person who doesn't believe everything we've told them."

Glancing at Carlos, I could see that the captain's statement had hit home. Crazy as it sounded, our neighbors *could* believe every word. Whenever you have some folks just barely making a living, and others living high on the hog, there has to be some ill feelings. Carlos had helped almost every family in the valley, including us, when we were all getting started, and some owed what little success they'd had to his generosity. But that didn't necessarily mean they weren't a bit jealous of him, and us too. We'd worked darned hard to turn an overgrazed prairie into a producing ranch, but some folks can't see beyond their noses. All they knew was we'd been halfway successful and they were still plugging away.

I tried to keep my voice natural when I spoke to him, but I ain't never been known for keeping my temper. My maw once said I was worse'n Paw when it come to getting mad. Still, there *are* times when a clear head is better, and this was a time like that. Believe me.

"Would your offer be likewise as far as me 'n' my family's concerned, Mr. Gresham? We ain't got much, I know, but it's all we have to our name. Far as cash goes, ain't none of us ever handled much, but I reckon a stake could git us a fresh start somewheres else. 'Course, I'd have to talk about it with my maw, and my brother Milo." Gresham nodded, sipping from his glass as he did. He looked sort of surprised.

"Would you mind tellin' me somethin', Mr. Gresham? Can't really hurt none, now you've got us where the hair is short and the woodbine twineth, as the poet once said. Tell me, are you really the land commissioner, and are these soldiers part of the U.S. Army? I know us Texans was on the side that lost the war, and we gotta understand why the Federals ain't very friendly, but how come you picked us for this takeover? Must be lots of other places where the land's a lot kinder and it's not so darned hard to work it. I'm jest sorta curious, you know, not tryin' to question what you're doin'. I sure gotta hand it to you. You're some slick article."

Gresham's eyes were a bit bloodshot, and his speech was somewhat thickened by the wine. He'd had much more to drink, it seemed, than any of us, and even now he was gesturing to the corporal to fill his glass.

"My boy," he said. "You're very young, and you have lots to learn about this modern day and age. Your very youth excuses you now, but time is a cruel taskmaster. I wasted my early years believing that all good things come to them as waits, like my father used to say. I took an active part in local politics, believing that my efforts on behalf of a candidate would earn its just reward.

"Well, it finally paid off. Would you believe I received this penny-ante position from a man who actually thought he was doing me a favor? He condemned me to this raw bit of frontier, thinking it would lead to better things. Well, he was certainly right. However, whatever success I have gained, I gained by myself. To answer one of your questions: I *am* the appointed land commissioner, for what that is worth.

"Colonel Dills's reward for many years of service was a written commendation and a monthly pension. Hardly enough to keep a bird alive, much less a man accustomed to living a full life. The other officers, including the captain here, got absolutely nothing, since they were not regular army. A militiaman signs up for varying periods. Most of these men that we have here had volunteered for one year.

"As the war continued, their enlistments were extended to another year, and another, and another. All this time, it seems, they were held in reserve. In *reserve,* mind you, for the entire duration of the war. They were forced to sit back in the rear while others went on to win promotions and the respect of their peers. So, as their families suffered from hunger back home, because the breadwinner was absent, my men were subject to army discipline, forced to participate in an endless series of marches and maneuvers—practice for a war they never even got to see. Does that sound fair to you?"

"Nossir," I replied. "It sure don't. I reckon I'd feel a lot like they did if I'd sat on my rear end for almost four years and had nothin' to show for it. But now, since we're not fightin' thet war no more, how come these fellers ain't back home with their families? How come they're still wearin' the uniforms and still actin' like soldiers? If it was me, I jest couldn't wait to shed them blues and git back to livin' like a human again."

A sly smile crossed his face, and he taken a sip of wine before answering my query. It was easy to guess what was on his mind, and I figgered to give him plenty of slack, enough so's he'd really open up and tell me what I needed to know. What it boiled down to, far as I could see, was that he felt he'd pulled off a darned clever trick and needed to brag a little bit. What satisfaction could come from planning and bringing off a big coup if nobody knew you had done it?

"I'd met the colonel in Washington while running errands for my friendly politico. On one occasion we were enjoying a dinner together, one paid for, incidentally, by that same ignorant politico. Toward the end of our meal he mentioned that he had volunteered his brigade for an important and strategic mission, a mission that could possibly bear heavily on the final outcome of the war. An inspection would be called in order to determine the brigade's capabilities in battle. The next day two high-ranking officers paid him a visit in his encampment and conducted the inspection.

"The whole affair took most of the day, and he was told a decision would be made within a week. Three days later he was called before the generals and told that his unit would not be satisfactory. The reason given was a ludicrous one." He cleared his throat noisily and swallowed before resuming his narrative.

"They were *over*trained. The men had gone through so many of those marches and maneuvers that they showed definite signs of battle fatigue. Can you imagine? Battle fatigue! Those who were questioned closely gave every indication of being battle weary, and they'd never heard a shot fired in anger.

"From my connections in Washington City, I knew the final outcome of the war would be victory for the North. Those in high places were well aware of the Rebels' problems. Supply was nigh impossible for units in the field. Ammunition was running very low, and food was almost gone. They would have to surrender, and soon. I also knew Union forces would need to occupy portions of the South for a long time after peace was declared, because of the inability of some to admit they were defeated. This meant an opportunity for a smart man.

"Before that evening was over I had explained my plan to the colonel and laid the groundwork for what you see here tonight. When my appointment as commissioner was confirmed, I simply forged orders from the War Department, transferring Dills's brigade to Texas as Reconstruction troops. Oh! One final bit of strategy was a note to the Secretary of War. In it I recommended that Camp Hudson be abandoned, as Indians and outlaws were no longer a problem in this area. To back up my suggestion, I enclosed another bit of forgery, a final report from a nonexistent scout troop, showing the problems as no longer dangerous. As you know, the troops were transferred to Fort Davis, and only a token force remains."

"By golly, Mr. Gresham! Like I said, I sure have to give you credit. You're one smart hombre. But tell me, are things really goin' like you figgered they would? Is there really an end in sight, like there should be? Seems you've sorta got yourself in a bind right now. You're holed up on this here ranch, and ain't able to do much of anything till my folks are accounted for. My brother Milo survived four years of that war you was talkin' about. Rode with a gent name of Bedford Forrest, and he's a real crackerjack at this sort of thing. It ain't gonna be easy, rootin' him out, and he might jest git mad enough to whip them 'battle weary' men of yours. Like the man said—don't be a-countin' chickens until they're clear of the eggs.

"And another thing," I added. "Don't be too sure of them other ranchers. There's a few of 'em that trailed north to Abilene with us, and they got their starts with wages that we paid them, plus the big bonuses they hadn't figgered on. Loyalty's a serious thing with Texas cowmen, and they might still figger to ride for our brand."

Gresham didn't like what I was saying—not even a little bit. I reckon he was beginning to realize that I was just leading him along, and this was one thing he'd never expected. At least not from a big, dumb country boy who'd acted like he didn't have sense enough to come in out of the rain.

He was becoming agitated, and his face was beet red. The corporal came forward with the bottle and filled his glass in response to a beckoning finger. The captain seemed to be unaware of what was being said, or just didn't care. He was leaning toward Esperanza, a smile on this thin face, gesturing with his hands as he told her something or other. Over on the other side of the table, Dills was staring morosely into his empty glass.

"Wellsir," I told Gresham. "You've answered me, I guess. Leastways, far as two of the questions go, you've given some straight answers. But tell me. How come you decided on the Val Verde? What was it that brought you to our valley? Like I said before, there's sure lots easier land available in other parts of Texas. Land with more water and a better soil." I put my hands together on the table and studied my oversized knuckles as I waited for him to reply.

Suddenly Gresham seemed to run out of patience. "I've told you enough!" he snapped. "Now you must decide whether or not you will accept my offer. I'll not press you for an answer. At least not tonight. Right now I'm tired, and I plan to retire." He finished the wine in his glass and put his hand over the top when the corporal stepped forward.

"No more, thank you," he told the man. "Go and call for the guards. These two men are ready to leave." He came to his feet stiffly and stared down at us. "I'll allow you until tomorrow to make your decisions," he told us. "After then, if your answer is not satisfactory, we will see what's to be done. I bid you good night, gentlemen."

The hair rose stiffly on the back of my neck. Suddenly all my assurance drained away, and I didn't know what the heck to do. For us to leave now, with Esperanza so closely involved with the captain, would be unthinkable. What could we do? What could *I* do, unless it would be to take on a lot more than one man could handle? That'd be just dumb, and I would probably wind up half crippled and unable to help the rest of my friends, much less my family.

Carlos must have been thinking along these same lines, I guess, 'cause he spoke right up. "My daughter is a young, unmarried woman," he told Gresham. "As is customary in our society, she must be accompanied by a guardian at all times. Usually this is an older, more experienced lady, and she is termed a *dueña*, a Spanish word that translates as chaperone or governess. I'm sure you will understand, Señor Gresham.

"The wife of one of my vaqueros filled this position before you occupied this ranch, but apparently she was confined with the other women. Since I've been told the women are more or less free now, I would greatly appreciate your having her summoned before we are taken away to our room. Her name is Señora Honrada, and she must be very concerned about the safety of her mistress. If you would be so kind, señor, as to do me this favor." His smile looked to be a grateful and appreciative one, but I knew he was burning inside.

In trying to play the gentleman, Gresham had led himself and the others between a rock and a hard place. Apparently, having the respect of Carlos was important to him, so he couldn't back-slide now. It had been real plain to me that he himself had some ideas about Esperanza and sure wasn't all that pleased with the captain's advances. He added some wrinkles to his brow before making up his mind.

"Corporal," he ordered. "Go to the women's quarters and bring back . . ." He swung around toward Carlos. "What did you say the woman's name was?" he asked. "Hurry, man. I'll honor your request, but it's late, and I'm very tired."

Carlos gave him the woman's name, and we settled back for a wait. I wasn't about to leave, with Esperanza helpless in the clutches of that bag-of-bones captain. She had the gun, but I wasn't all that sure she'd be ready to kill a man.

Reaching forward, I felt the side of a coffeepot. Not as hot as I'd like it to be, but it was better than none at all. I offered some to Carlos, and he held up his cup with a grateful smile. Gresham shook his head.

"I wouldn't be able to sleep," he told me. He did look a bit tired, and I doubted the coffee would make a difference.

"What's gonna happen to all these men?" I asked him. "Do you plan on portionin' out this land to them, or what? Will they jest stay on and work for you, or will they strike out on their own? You know, it takes a lot of this graze for a beef critter to jest git by, and if you're plannin' on bein' in the cattle business, you'll need all you can hang on to."

"I told you I'd answered all the questions I intend to," he said waspishly. "Can't you get it through your head to shut that mouth for a while? You're skating on thin ice."

"Uh, sorry," I told him. "Jest tryin' to make your waitin' easier. Talkin' about waitin'," I went on, "have you ever been all by your lonesome somewheres? Mebbe where the darkness was so black you could almost cut it? Way out in the middle of nowhere, alone and scared, and you jest knowed thet someone, or some*thing,* was out there in the dark, but you couldn't see it, or even really know jest *where* it could be. You started to sweat, even though the night was cool, and then shivers started shakin' your whole body. The hairs on the back of your neck raised up, and you could sense thet critter, or mebbe a man, was

comin' to grab you. You're not able to move, 'cause your muscles are like water. You—''

''What on earth are you jabbering about, McCowan?''
Gresham was close to the edge: I could see that. His bloodshot
eyes shifted nervously as he stared around the room, and he had
a tic starting at one corner of his mouth. ''What nonsense! Rav-
ing about strange things in the night! What are you trying to do?
Test my nerve?'' That tic was really jumping.

''Not at all, Mr. Gresham,'' I told him. ''It's jest thet I got to
thinkin', and I figgered I'd better let you know. Us McCowans
is part Injun, you know, and we got us a whole pile of Injuns
related to our family. Injuns is sure enough bad medicine when
they git a score agin you. Paw used to say Injuns don't git mad;
they jest gits even.

''Ain't no reasonin' with 'em, once they start after somebody. They'll stay on a trail till they drop, and when one does
drop, there's always a dozen to take his place. I sure don't mean
all this as threats, Mr. Gresham. I was jest being honest with
you. Why, some of them could be out there right now, creepin'
around, tryin' to figger where to start thet revenge—killin' and
takin' scalps so's they can ride on home and tell the others
they've evened that score. The average Injun's got a real lust
for blood, you know. I heard tell there ain't nothin' an Injun'd
ruther do than cut out a feller's heart and jest plain waller
around in his blood. What was *thet*, Gresham? Thought I heard
a noise. There, by thet window. Sort of a scratchin' sound.
Didn't you hear nothin' at all? Oh, I forgot. You're a city feller,
and you can't hear things like us country boys. Listen. There it
is again. Like mebbe somebody with a knife, pryin' at a
windowsill.''

Whatever Gresham might have had to say, he didn't, 'cause
that Señora what's-her-name came in about then. Reckon she
really had been worried about Esperanza, 'cause she ran over to
where we were sitting and pulled Esperanza to her feet.

Paying no mind to the rest of us, she latched on to Esperanza
and wrapped an arm around her, urging her toward that doorway, shoving folks aside, all the while spouting the darnedest
batch of Mex talk you ever did hear. Parts of what she was say-

ing were sweet, endearing words, but some of them others gave me the idea that she was plenty mad. I had the time of my life trying to keep from laughing out loud. The captain wasn't all that sure as to what had happened. He'd tried to hang on to Esperanza, but thet old lady just plunked him back down in his chair. Now he was asking Gresham what was going on, and his boss was too aggravated to explain.

"Shut up!" Gresham was trembling with fury as he turned and glared at me. "Don't think for a moment that I haven't been aware of your intentions, McCowan. You and your bumpkin philosophy! Let your dirty Indians come, and we'll make them wish they'd never been born. My men are more than sufficient to defeat the whole tribe, and believe me, sir, your heels will be dancing on air before the first shot is fired at them. Now get out of my sight before I change my mind. Corporal! Bring in the guards, and take them away!" He put one hand up to his eyes, rubbed them, and sat down. Worried by all the fuss but not knowing just what had happened, the captain tried to calm him.

As the guards went about strapping Carlos in the chair, I tried to make out what was being said, but they were too far away for me to hear clearly. I did hear my name mentioned, and caught the words "valuable" and "success." Whatever it was, I was convinced it meant nothing good for us.

It was a sure enough dark night, with no sign of a moon, and high clouds blotting out the stars. A guard bumped into another and cursed him savagely. It was close to the dark I'd described to Gresham, and remembering his angry face, I couldn't help chuckling.

"What's so damn funny?" the clumsy guard snarled. "Ain't nothing to laugh about. Man can't see his hand in front of his face on a night like this."

I reckoned that baiting Gresham *had* been a silly move on my part, but I hadn't been able to resist doing it. All the high cards seemed to be in his hand right now, and anything that could chip away at his confidence was worth trying. A step in the right direction, you might say. Besides, being new to the border country, he was ready to believe most anything. Under all his bluster, he'd shown naked fear.

The leading chair carrier walked into a pillar and nearly fell. The chair tilted dangerously, and I grabbed the back to steady it. It was the fat guard, and he complained about being worked too hard. It was easy to see that morale was low among these men, and it wouldn't take much to cause consternation, and eventually panic. Might be smart to keep on telling my stories, and make them even bloodier.

When we arrived at the door to Carlos's room, one of them groped his way inside and lighted a lamp. I watched as he walked curiously about the room, inspecting the paintings and statuary. He held the lamp above his head and paused a moment before each work of art. I held my breath for a long minute when he fingered one of the carved oak panels next to the one that opened into the secret passage.

"This here place's like a museum," he commented. "I sure do appreciate nice things. Always wished I could have me my own room back home, instead of sharing it with three brothers. 'Course, I'd never been able to collect stuff like he has here, but I had some Injun arrowheads, and an old drum my grandpap thumped on back during the Revolution." He set the lamp down on the nightstand, and I let out the breath in relief.

"Bring him on in," he told the others. "Be careful now. Don't be banging into none of that furniture. I swear, the way you men act I'd think you were born in a barn."

He helped as they unbuckled the strap and lifted Carlos onto his bed. "There now," he said. "Can you take care of yourself from here on? If so, we'll be on our way."

Carlos nodded, somewhat surprised at the man's politeness and courtesy, as was I. He thanked the soldier and started to unbutton his coat, loosening his tie with the other hand.

I was standing just inside the door, and as they shuffled past, one of the men bumped into me. I felt something heavy drop into my coat pocket and wondered what it could be.

"Well, good night," the polite soldier told me. "Hope you have a good rest. You might have the doc take a look at the wound on your arm and make sure it's healing proper."

"Thanks," I said. "Mebbe I'll do jest thet. Didn't know you fellers had a doctor with you. Does he know his stuff?"

One guard laughed. "Yeah," he replied. "That is, when he ain't drunker'n a skunk, which is most of the time."

I waved, and locked the door behind them. Waiting until I was sure they'd gone, I reached down into the coat pocket and drew out a pepperbox pistol. An English make, it was an older gun but appeared to be in good shape. About .36 caliber, I figgered, it was fully loaded and capped. Huh? It purely didn't make sense. Who had put the gun in my pocket, and why would he do it? I walked over to the bed.

"Lookee here, Carlos. One of those soldiers left me this here gun. Dropped it in my pocket as they were passin' out the door. Now, why would one of them want to help us? Jest don't make any sense, does it?"

He agreed, but told me not to question the man's motives. "For whatever reason, he has done us a favor," he said. "It could easily mean the difference between life and death for us. Can you conceal it in your clothing? Somewhere so you can reach it in a hurry? Certainly couldn't help us hidden in this room. It must be close at hand when we need it."

I thought for a moment. "I *could* hang it on a piece of leather thong and drape it around my neck. I doubt they're gonna search us anymore, and I could sure git it out in no time at all. You got some latigo or mebbe a whang lace in this room? Somethin' limber enough so's it won't chafe my neck? I know! How's about usin' thet cord off your sombrero? It would do the trick jest fine, and it's about the right length, so I won't have to cut it none."

Carlos told me to help myself. "It doesn't seem that I will be doing any riding, Lyse. At least not for a while."

So that's what I done. It did work, just fine, and made a big difference in my attitude. Now I didn't feel quite so trapped, like before. If it came to a showdown, I'd take out Gresham and the captain before I started in on some of the others. By that time we'd have some more guns, and our chances would be that much better. I even felt cheerful as I bedded down and told Carlos good night.

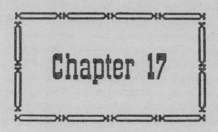

Chapter 17

They woke us early the next morning. The false light of
dawn was barely coloring the skies when the loud banging
at the door brought me out of my sound sleep. The bedroll
I'd spread on the floor had been comfortable enough, and I felt
pretty good, all things considered. I glanced at Carlos, on his
back in the heavy oaken bed, and saw he was stirring.

"I reckon you're awake," I said, sitting up on my pallet.
Carlos had recommended the settee, but nothing that fragile
could ever support my frame, and I'd told him so. Rising to my
feet, I padded over to the door and unlocked it. One of our
guards stood just outside, the one who'd disarmed my fat friend

the night before. "They want you to hurry," he told me. "They're waiting out by the corrals."

"Thanks," I answered. "I gotta help Don Carlos up first off, then we'll need somebody to carry his chair. Shouldn't take more'n fifteen minutes for him to git hisself dressed. Why don't you come back about then and bring some others?"

He nodded but made no effort to leave. It seemed to me that mebbe he had something on his mind. Something he wanted to say but wasn't all that sure of how to go about it.

"Did you want to tell me more, soldier?" I asked. "You'd might as well spit it out, 'cause I ain't no mind reader."

He glanced to each side uneasily. "Yeah," he muttered. "There is something, but I ain't sure I can trust you. Maybe we could just step inside the room, so's the whole state of Texas can't hear what we're saying. That all right?"

I shrugged. "It's fine by me, soldier, but ain't you a little afraid? I might jest take thet gun away and escape. How would you explain *that* to your boss man?"

He grinned. "I doubt that," he told me. "How would *he* run away?" He pointed across the room at Carlos, then suddenly sobered. "I didn't mean anything disrespectful. Honest I didn't. I don't poke fun at a man just because he limps, or can't walk at all. I saw too many men come back from the war with arms and legs gone. That can happen to anybody."

"All right," I told him. "You made your point. Now, you had somethin' you wanted to say, so let's hear it."

"Well," he began, "I didn't know what I was getting into when I agreed to come along on this little adventure. I had no idea there was gonna be a lot of killing, and especially killing women and kids. That's what he's got in mind, and I can't go along with that. Gresham's a crazy man, and he's a whole lot crazier than most realize. He knows that he must kill you all or he'll be looking over his shoulder for the rest of his life. There'd be no way he could ever relax or enjoy this good life he's laid out for himself."

He leaned his rifle against the wall and took out a sack of tobacco. "Mind if I smoke?" he asked. "I ain't got time to tell you the whole story, but I'll do my best. You go on and get yourselves dressed, and I'll keep an eye out for the rest of the guards. They were still stuffing their faces in the kitchen, so I doubt they'll be along for a while.

"First," he said, "did you hide that little gun I dropped in your pocket last night? Have you got it somewheres so you can pull it out when it's needful? Just say yes or no. Don't bother telling me where you have it. I'd rather not even know. You have? Fine. That's real fine. To tell the truth, I was afraid you might muff it. Might be startled when you felt it drop in your pocket and give us away."

He scratched a match alight on his thumbnail and lit his cigarette. Taking a couple of big drags, he began to tell his tale.

"Like I said before, I ain't exactly a saint, but I don't hold with killing women and kids, or helpless men either, if they got no way to fight back. When I agreed to go along on his big land grab, I had no idea that he'd planned to kill a bunch of folks. He told us the whole thing wouldn't take no more'n a week. That you people didn't have any guns, 'cause the Army had taken them all away. Said we'd just come on in here, use his forged papers to confiscate the property, then escort everybody across the Mexican border. Even said you'd be given money, so's you could make a new start over there.

"One of the other fellows heard him make you an offer to do pretty much what I've just told you. Don't you believe a word that he says! As soon as you sign any legal papers, I guarantee, you're as good as dead. I don't know how he figures to do it, but he'll find a way. The troop that planned to attack your ranch, McCowan, has a Gatling rapid-fire gun and enough ammunition to fight another war. It could be he intends to use that gun to do the killings. I don't know."

I gazed at him curiously. "I sure do appreciate what you're tellin' us," I told him. "We'd already figgered that as Gresham's plan, but it does help to know exactly where we stand. Howsomever, why are you stickin' around if you want no part in the killins? Why don't you jest saddle a horse and git the heck outta here?"

He pinched out that cigarette and rubbed the back of his neck absentmindedly. He shrugged. "I'll be damned if I know, Mc-

Cowan. If I did leave, I'd have it on my mind for the rest of my life. Man's gotta live with himself, you know. Trouble is, I can't see how me staying around is gonna make a real difference. There's too darn many others to contend with. Men who count on every word that Gresham told them, and some who don't believe but really don't care *what* has to be done, so long as they get their share. I'm sure a number of the men feel as I do, but they're in the minority, and I wouldn't even know where to begin looking for them."

"Listen to me," I told him. "We ain't so helpless as it might seem. I ain't gonna say exactly why, but you can sure believe me when I tell you this." I sized him up just a bit more closely and decided to go on.

"The only way Gresham could force the vaqueros to come in here and free Dills's bunch was by tellin' 'em me 'n' Vargas would be shot, or mebbe even hanged. Wellsir, they did what he asked, all right, but not before one of 'em managed to be long gone and on his way after some help. There was plenty of vaqueros out in the line camps; four of 'em was over in Sycamore Canyon, along with a half-Apache cook, and you can jest bet your last peso that's where he headed.

"Right now there's prob'ly a dozen or more out there, jest waitin' for the right time to attack without riskin' a chance of us gittin' killed. Then there's mebbe a few more burnin' leather to our friends, lettin' 'em know jest what's been goin' on here. Heck, if the truth was known, they jest might be comin' in and outta here every night, 'cause every Mexican looks the same to these here gringos."

He stared. "If that's true," he said, "then I'll be in just as much danger as any of the rest." He paused. "It does seem pretty farfetched," he said. "After all, we have over a hundred men here at the ranch, and another sixty are out at your place. Every trooper is well armed, and after a training period of four years, they are almost all very good marksmen. No, I think it would take more than a few irate Mexicans to win back this ranch. You'd best think of another way. Something you can count on." A thought struck him, and he suddenly looked alarmed.

"Hey! We've been gabbing away here like a couple of old women. Like I said, they were in a hurry, and wanted you to come right away. You finish getting dressed, and I'll fetch two more men to carry the chair. Don't lose heart, though, because I'll help in any way I can." Grabbing up his rifle, he dashed through the door.

"How about you, Carlos?" I called out. "Can you use some help there. I'm about ready myself."

"I also," he replied. "While you were conversing with our new friend I managed to dress myself. However, I could use a hand with these boots, if you don't mind, Lyse."

I helped him to prop himself against the head of the bed and pull on the boots. "Tell me, what do you think of our friend?" he asked. "He sounds very sincere, and appears to really want to help us. Can we trust him, do you think? It might mean a great deal if we knew for certain."

I shrugged. "Who can say for sure. Like you said, he sounds sincere enough. Thinkin' logically, the chances of Gresham sendin' somebody to spy on us don't make sense. He's already got us way outnumbered, and he and the others are so darn sure of themselves they prob'ly haven't even considered we'd try to win back this place. To escape—thet's a foregone conclusion. He *knows* we might try to run, but he's darned sure that his guards can stop us. No, thet feller's one hundred percent. I'd stake my life on it. And I reckon thet's what I'll be doin'," I added with a grin.

At the washstand I ran some water into the basin, washed my face and hands, and combed my hair as best I could. The cowlick I'd been cursed with since I was just a little feller gave me the usual amount of trouble, but I plastered it down with water. Carlos thanked me when I brought over the basin and a towel.

"Ah," he said. "I really do miss Poco Luce. He was able to help me in so many ways. Not only in simple things like this, but he was also a fine listener. And," he added, "he had little to say in return. I shouldn't say that in jest, but I know you must understand. I sometimes thought of him as I would my son, even though he was somewhat grotesque in appearance. He had the face of a gargoyle, but his soul was pure as an angel's. He loved me like he would a father—to such a degree that he would lay down his life for me. And I was forced to watch them kill him. They shot him down as a man would kill an animal, and they continued to shoot long after he was dead. Man is a perverse creature, Lysander. He destroys more than he creates, and although he knows that what he does is wrong, his petulance and obstinacy will not allow him to admit this, even to himself. This man, Gresham, is a greedy, grasping misfit, and his desire for money and power, no matter what he has to do to attain it, is a classic example of how far a man can sink morally. He *must* be destroyed—he and all those with him who follow the same principles, or rather the lack of them. No matter the cost, we've an obligation to kill them all.''

The sound of footsteps interrupted whatever I might have had to say in reply. I reckoned it was just as well, since there wasn't much I could have added. Carlos knew how I was feeling, and also knew I'd do my best to kill Gresham.

The fat guard wasn't along this time, but our friend was back, and he directed the others in lifting Carlos and putting him in the chair. Again he cautioned them about bumping into the furniture and made sure they were gentle with Carlos. The new man seemed to be trying to catch my eye as he bent over the chair, and he seemed familiar to me. Then I placed him. It was that corporal who had served the wine the night before, only now his chevrons were gone. A darker patch showed on both sleeves, with threads dangling from the cloth. Looking closer, I saw that his left eye was swollen, and a dark, purple blotch covered that side of his face. He had been badly used by someone, and I had me an idea that it might've been Gresham, since the stripes were gone. Gresham was a small man, and apparently he had a small man's complex about getting even. I wondered. Last night it had showed up with that nervous twitch at the side of his mouth, a sure sign of complete frustration. He hadn't dared to touch me, because he knew I wouldn't stop until his men had killed me. He needed me and didn't want me dead—not yet. It looked as if someone had smacked this man around, knowing he couldn't risk fighting back. Only a low coward would pull a stunt like that.

As I watched, the man glanced around, then fixed his eyes on me and struck himself lightly over the heart with his right hand. He repeated this twice again, as though he had meant it to be a signal of some sort, then looked away.

Now, with Indians this meant "friend," used sometimes to show friendship or to indicate the telling of truths. We'd learned this from Paw when we were just younkers. But how would this Yankee soldier know about things like this? Before I had time to consider it further, they were already on their way out with Carlos, and me 'n' that friendly guard were tagging along behind.

Halfway to the corrals he stopped and lifted one of his boots as if to examine the sole. In a whisper he told how Gresham had roughed up the corporal after we'd left for our room. "I think he might be a ready candidate for our side," he told me. "Right now he'd likely shoot Gresham himself if he thought he could get away with it. I haven't had much chance to talk to him, but I know he's mad. Really mad. He never cared much for being a dog robber—that's the name we put on a soldier who picks up after an officer and polishes his boots. Even worse when a man has to wait on a lousy civilian. His name is Solamon, Mort Solamon, but the others have been joshing him and calling him Sally."

I nodded as we walked around the rear of the building. "I can understand how he feels, all right. I couldn't stand any part of a job like thet. Talk to him if you can find a chance, but play it smart. Don't give yourself away."

I stared as we came in sight of the corrals. Gresham, a cigar jutting from his mouth, was sitting in that chair of Carlos's, which he apparently had made some soldier drag out of the dining room. Dills was standing alongside, but the captain was nowhere in sight. A pair of barebacked horses, their halters held by soldiers, stood in front of the barn's entrance, and two long ropes dangled from the ridgepole. A noose had been tied on one end, and three big soldiers held on to the other. From their smiles, I figgered they were not unwilling to do their job. Probably volunteered.

"Well. Good morning, gentlemen." Gresham looked a little the worse for wear. His eyes were puffy, and dark bags sagged underneath. His smile seemed forced, and his manner was very nervous as he fidgeted with the buttons on his coat.

"I assume you have discussed our little proposition, so I would like to hear your answers here and now. Tell me, can I count on your signatures this morning? I have the papers right here, all clear and properly drawn, so there shouldn't be any hesitation on your part. You may read them, if that is your pleasure, but I assure you it isn't necessary. After all, you really have no alternatives." He giggled.

Reaching into a shirt pocket, I taken out my tobacco and built me a smoke. Carlos sat back in his chair, facing to the east, where long fingers of reddish-orange light reached up through ragged clouds, turning the snowy white to graying blacks and browns as the sun's rim reached the horizon. He said nothing, nor did I.

Flies flew their vigil over manure piles; a horse stamped a hoof, and the skin on his flank rippled loosely; ranks of uniformed soldiers stood at ease, each with his right toe in back of his left heel. One hawked and spat noisily.

"Well?" demanded Gresham. "What's it to be? Come, come, you two. Let's hear your answers."

I licked the paper's edge and rolled it tightly, twisting one end and placing the other in my mouth. It jiggled as I gave him my answer. "Go to hell, Gresham. I pass."

While Gresham was still choking on that one, Carlos spoke his little piece. "I really don't feel that you deserve a reply," he said, "much less an explanation. But I will let you listen to mine.

"My family's blood has soaked this ground on which we're gathered. They fought Indians, and ran an invading Mexican usurper, López de Santa Anna, clear out of Texas. Once before we had a greedy man such as you who sought to claim a part of this land. His name was Shaler, and his bones lie moldering in the Indian Nations. We didn't give in to him, and we are not about to make an agreement with a scoundrel such as you have shown yourself to be. Never!

"One more thing. You may feel secure with your army of turncoats such as the colonel there. But beware! At this very moment, riders are closing on this ranch with anger in their hearts and guns in their hands. You will never live to enjoy this ranch. Tell me, señor! Have you ever watched a man dragged by a horse across the *barrancas*—this broken, flintlike expanse of land to the south? Believe me, even a mother would fail to recognize what remained as her son."

He sat up straighter in the chair. "Whatever you plan, please get on with it. I have no patience with cowards."

For a long moment Gresham just sat there, not speaking. His face was almost purple, and he tore at his collar, loosening the button and clawing at his cravat. "You'll wish you'd never opened your big mouth, you self-righteous boor!" He almost screamed the words as he glared at Carlos.

Turning, he shouted to a sergeant standing by the barn doors. "Bring that foreman out here right now! I'll show you what you've caused by your filthy, lying insults, you . . . you . . . greaser! I'll make you crawl, and beg to sign this paper!"

Playing it safe, he had four men tie my hands behind me. I reckon he knew that I'd never stand still for what he had planned to do if we refused to sign the documents. I tried to fight them off, but they'd taken me by surprise, and that wound in my arm didn't help much.

I watched the blood drain from Carlos's face and saw him grip the arms of his chair until the knuckles stood whitened by the strain. It was Miguel Vargas that the others led from the barn, blood still dripping from a gash on his head and his arms bound behind his back. A soldier kicked at his rump, and Miguel stumbled and fell helplessly. They jerked him to his feet and shoved him toward the two bareback horses standing under the noosed ropes.

While one soldier held the halter, several others boosted Vargas onto the back of one of the horses. Vargas was a big man, and it took four men to get the job done. His brown, weathered face was impassive, and he looked to neither the right nor left as a sergeant slipped the noose around his neck and adjusted the knot behind his ear. Satisfied, he stepped back, one arm raised in preparation for the signal, then grunted and fell facedown, a bone-handled knife standing out from his back.

A shotgun roared, and the four who'd lifted Vargas were smashed to the ground. The frightened horse reared, and the man holding the halter lost his grip, allowing the terrified animal to bolt.

Vargas hung for a moment as the horse ran out from under him, then fell and rolled on the ground, the noose still on his neck. Thank God the soldiers holding the free end had not held on tight, and Miguel wasn't dead.

I could hear a strange sound, and it was becoming louder: high-pitched voices shrieking something over and over, the words not too clear. Then a mob of women came running out from behind one of the bunkhouses, pitchforks, scythes, hoes, and bright machetes waving in the air. *"A la muerte,"* they were screaming. *"A la muerte! A la muerte!"* To the death!

Most of Gresham's men were unarmed, and many died in that first onslaught. Bunching up like sheep, the terrified few that survived did so only because they were lying under the others who were already dead. The women hacked at many as they ran for their lives, screaming for mercy.

Fighting to get my hands free of the ropes, I saw Gresham leap to his feet, eyes staring in terror, his mouth slack, a dribble of saliva running down his chin. He stood there an instant, then turned to run, but Carlos was too quick. He'd somehow lunged from his chair and clutched Gresham's throat in his hands. They rolled on the ground as soldiers trying to escape from the women hid them from view.

"Cut these durn ropes!" I was hollering, fighting through the press of maddened women. The noise was unbelievable, a blending of the men's screams and the women's war cry that made it impossible to understand words. The mob surged over what soldiers were left alive, hacking relentlessly with the razor-edged farm tools as their victims begged them to stop the killings. Grimly the women continued to cut and slash, ignoring upraised arms and pleas for mercy. Recognizing me from my size, a big, fat lady stopped long enough to cut my hands free with one of the two butcher knives she wielded in bloody fists. I thanked her, then ran to where I'd last seen Miguel Vargas.

Lancelot Gilkie was already there, his shotgun lying beside him and the big LeMat hanging from its sling. Vargas was sitting up, rubbing his neck where a raw, reddened mark was plainly visible. "Well, little brother," he said. "That is as close as I ever want to come to dying. I could feel the Angel of Death breathing in my ear."

"Yeah," I told him. "But it ain't over, not jest yet. I need a gun, Mr. Gilkie." I pointed to the shotgun. "Thet thing loaded?" Mr. Gilkie shook his head but handed me his powder flask and a leather bag filled with buckshot.

"The caps are in thet patchbox, in the stock," he said to me, grinning as he surveyed the battlefield. "Well? Ain't thet some army I got there? I told you them women were all primed to fight! They're mean, ain't they? No monkey business with them. They'll cut a man's guts out and not even blink an eye! Oh, sure, after it's all over they'll mebbe cry some and wonder what ever made 'em do it, but they'd do it all over again if you fooled with their kin. Let me—"

A burst of rifle shots cut short his words. The soldiers in the towers had gotten over their fright and were laying down a heavy fire. One bullet hit the dirt next to Vargas, and another put a hole through Mr. Gilkie's hat. One of the women screamed in pain and fell, blood staining her blouse as it poured from a wound in her shoulder.

Unable to fight the towers with nothing more than tools, the rest of the women were taking shelter wherever it could be found. A few picked up rifles where scared soldiers had dropped them, and returned the fire until the magazines ran dry. A pair of brave women left their cover and ran out to ransack bodies for more ammunition. One, hit in the thigh, dragged herself back to the shelter of the barn with a belt of cartridges clutched in her hand. Another, her arms filled with belts, was shot down in her tracks and died there.

"Into the barn!" I hollered. "C'mon, you two. Haul your

rear ends into thet barn. I'm gonna try 'n' find Carlos, then fetch him over there. See if you can't give them women some help whilst you're in there. Keep them guards' heads down, so's they can't kill no more of them gals.''

Crouching in the lee of the barn, I charged both barrels and capped the shotgun. The pepperbox was still dangling around my neck, although, to tell the truth, I'd forgotten it was there. Miguel was just inside the barn door, and I tossed him the gun. "Here," I yelled. "See if you can do some good with thet." A moment later I heard the unmistakable bark of Mr. Gilkie's LeMat and the sharp crack of the small-caliber pepperbox. Neither was much good at far range, but they might serve to make the guards somewhat cautious.

The rifle fire *was* letting up, and I peered around at the towers. There was a large horse trough near where I had last seen Carlos, so I gathered my legs under me and charged over there, flinging myself down behind the trough. Around me a number of soldiers lay dead, some badly mutilated. One wore a .44 Army Colt in a holster, with a cartridge pouch on his belt. After retrieving the revolver I looked in the pouch and found two packages of skin cartridges, paper-wrapped for quick loading. Checking the gun, I found it fully loaded.

Now I had something with a little range to it. A shotgun was murderous at close range, but it wouldn't reach out very darn far. The Colt was fairly accurate up to about a hundred yards, and its big, heavy bullet packed one heck of a wallop. The nearest tower was no further away than thet, and it presented an easy target.

Hollering over to Vargas in Spanish, I asked him to show himself just enough so's the fellers in the tower might be tempted to try a crack at him. *"Tienes cuidado,"* I cautioned him, rubbing my sweaty palms on my pants.

Sure enough, two of them raised up and started firing at him. Cocking the Colt, I taken careful aim and fired. A split second later I let go the second round and scored on both of them. One stood up, swayed, and fell to the ground. The other slumped back into the boxlike structure.

Feeling certain the tower was no longer dangerous, I left the shelter of the water trough and found Carlos lying just where I'd figgered he'd be. Gresham's body lay next to him, dead or unconscious. Carlos grinned and spoke to me.

"I wondered when you would come for me? Silly, isn't it? A grown man, and here I am, completely helpless. I might've crawled, I suppose, but I hesitated to leave the shelter. A very discouraging situation, being disabled at such a time!" Reaching over, he grabbed a handful of Gresham's shirtfront.

"He's not dead, Lyse. I came close to killing him, but I would rather see him hang, wouldn't you? Of course, if we lose this fight, we can always put a bullet into him before we're recaptured." Gresham's eyes were closed, and he sure looked as if he'd been through a wringer. I pulled his limp form erect and slung him over my shoulder.

"I'll be right back, amigo. Here, take this here gun. I gotta have some help packing you to the barn, so I'll fetch somebody back with me. There's three shots left in it, and here's some more loads." I handed him the skin cartridges.

There was a real surprise waiting in the barn. My old buddy, the friendly guard, was there, along with the corporal who'd been busted by Gresham. Both were stripped to the waist and wore red neckerchiefs wrapped around their foreheads. Somehow, they'd found some *algodones* to wear—white cotton trousers worn by native laborers, with cuffs tied at the bottoms and wide leather waist belts. Each had a rifle slung over his shoulder, a machete on his belt, and a bandolier of ammunition around his neck—something we could use.

"Here," I told them. "I got a present for you." I let go of Gresham, and he sprawled unconscious in the dirt. "I'd be obliged if one of you would give me a hand with Carlos. He's the one thet·caught this here weasel and deserves some credit for a job well done. I left him over there behind a horse trough, 'cause I couldn't carry 'em both. Give one of them bandoliers to those gals over there. They got a rifle or two but no more cartridges. They can help cover us."

They both volunteered, and we had no trouble fetching him back to the barn. Sally, or Solamon, spotted his chair and dragged it along. Once there, we sat Carlos down in it and started figgering what we'd do next.

"We don't have enough guns to arm all the women, nor much ammunition for the few guns we got." It was Mr. Gilkie who started the council, and his face wore a serious frown. "If we don't come up with a plan soon, it'll be too late. They still outnumber us over two to one, and they all have guns. There's the six of us, counting Don Carlos, and twenty women are still on their feet. I counted over thirty dead men in the wagon yard, and there's mebbe a few more thet're cut up enough so's they ain't much use as fighters. They had over a hundred men when all this ruckus started, meanin' we have about seventy of 'em to lick if we're to git out of this in one piece. Anybody got any ideas?"

"Before we do anything," Carlos said earnestly, "we must try to free my vaqueros. The women have done their part, in a way I prayed wouldn't be necessary, but their bravery gives us a chance we would never have had. Now let's free their men, which is what they were really fighting for after all. In any event, my men can make better use of the guns. After all, most of them are excellent marksmen. If it comes down to a hand-to-hand fight, they will fight like demons. Also, with the thirty-four vaqueros we'll even our odds."

"Don Carlos is right," I agreed. "Okay, here's what will have to be done. I'm the youngest, and though I ain't all thet fast on my feet, I do pack the weight it'll take if we have to break down the doors. The rest of you git over with them women and lay down some coverin' fire when I'm ready. I watched when them fellers were runnin' from the gals, and most of 'em headed for thet bunch of cottonwoods on the far side of the bunkhouses. About now they might be gittin' in shape to charge us, so this'll have to be done real fast. I reckon that's about all I got to say."

"I'm going along with you." It was my friendly guard, in his ridiculous getup, looking like one of them pirates you read about in history books. "There are two bunkhouses we have to break into," he told us, "and it'll take two men, if time is short, as you've said. I maybe don't weigh as much as you, but I *can* run. Besides, I want to do my part.''

I shrugged. ''Well, it's all right by me, if you really want to come along. You know, it jest occurred to me—we don't even know your name! What is it?—jest in case we have to carve somethin' on your grave marker, God forbid.''

''Why, I'm Mayhew,'' he replied. ''Archibald Mayhew. Known to my friends as Arch.'' He handed his rifle to Mr. Gilkie, along with the bandolier of ammunition.

''I'll just hang on to this machete,'' he said. ''If we get into a fight, I'll need more than just my fists, I'm sure.''

Going to a window that faced toward the bunkhouses some sixty yards away, I peered out of one corner. Bodies littered the ground, but I couldn't see anyone moving around.

''C'mon,'' I told Mayhew. ''Let's git this over with. Don't try nothin' fancy, you hear? Once we git them doors opened, turn around and run fast as you can. I'll be jest behind you. Watch you don't git trampled in the rush. Them mad vaqueros are gonna be in some kind of a hurry too.''

We crouched just inside the big door, and I raised up an arm. ''Now!'' I hollered as I dropped my arm. ''Let's go!''

To one side of us, the others started firing as rapidly as they could work the levers. To me those bunkhouses were a mile away, or so it seemed. Dodging the bodies, and jumping over some, we reached the shelter of the buildings. The windows had all been boarded up, and two huge padlocks were locked on hasps that had been bolted to doors and frames.

In Spanish I told those inside to stand back, and lunged against the door with my shoulder, holding one arm across my chest. It sagged inward but didn't give one inch. Wishing I had brought along a bar of some kind, I smashed into that door again, and it still wouldn't give. Then, realizing it opened outward, and I was competing with its frame as well as the locks, I transferred my attention to the windows.

The boards were rough-sawn two-by-tens, and whoever installed them had used plenty of nails. Taking a grip on an end, I stuck my foot up on the wall and pulled hard. With a screech of protest the nails gradually began to loosen and come free.

Once I'd gotten that first board off, the others weren't nearly so hard to rip loose. After the second, the vaqueros began helping me, smashing out the glass and kicking at the boards with their feet. Minutes later they began climbing out, and I quickly explained what they must do.

"The barn," I said. "You boys run like you've never run before, and try not to git hit. I'll be along darn quick."

Arch was having trouble. I could see that. He hadn't had any luck with the door, but he was still trying, kicking the locks with his boot. I showed him what had to be done and hollered to the men inside to break out the glass and help all they could. Didn't take more'n a minute, and we had 'em all out of there and headed for the barn, where the lessening of the cover fire warned me that ammunition must be low.

Someone—it sounded like Vargas—was hollering at us, and it sounded urgent, though I couldn't make out the words. In front of us I could see that one of the vaqueros had gotten hit and was dragging a leg, helped by one of the others. A moment later they reached the barn and dodged inside.

"Let's git!" I told Mayhew. "We done what we came to do here. Run, Arch. Run like the Devil's at your heels."

He taken off, with me just behind. Halfway there I felt a bullet tug at my pants leg, and Mayhew jerked and stumbled, then fell sprawling to the ground. I knelt down next to him and saw a thumb-sized hole just above his belt. It was centered on his backbone. I started to lift him, but he cried out, "Don't, please! My guts are blown out. Leave me be, Lyse. I'm gonna die anyway, so save yourself. Just get going, and let me die in peace. Can't move my legs, and that means my back's broke." He looked up at me. "Honest, Lyse. It don't hurt none. I can't feel a thing. Don't you blame yourself, Lyse. It's maybe better this way. You see to it that Gresham hangs, will you? Promise me, Lyse!" He stared wide-eyed, his grin slowly fading. . . . He was gone.

A bullet clipped the ground next to me, and another went past my ear. The barrage from the barn increased, and a man screamed in pain behind me. They were close. I leaped up and ran bent over as fast as I could. A slug just skinned the point of my shoulder, smarting but not really hurting a whole lot. Another bullet grazed my side, and then I reached the barn and slipped through the door.

"You all right, McCowan?" It was Solamon, and he grabbed my arm. "Here," he said. "Have a swig of this." He handed me a dark bottle with the cork out.

"It's brandy," he told me. "I swiped it from Gresham. I thought maybe it just might come in handy."

I taken a long swallow and felt the warmth spreading all through my body. "Thanks," I told him, handing it back. "I thank you very much. Mayhew's dead. I guess you saw that. Bullet caught him right in the middle of his back."

Before he could comment on that, Miguel Vargas ran over, his face sweating and powder-streaked. "We're just about out of ammunition, little brother! Another dozen rounds or so and we'll be using those rifles as clubs. What'll we do for more cartridges, Lyse? You got any ideas, or a plan?"

"Yeah," I told him. "I don't guarantee it'll work, but I figger we can't lose nothin' by tryin'. Mr. Gilkie tells me there's three Winchesters, and about five hundred cartridges to fit, in that secret room right off the patio. I'll make a try for it if you can figger a way to keep them off of my back for a minute or two. It'll be risky, but I figger you can mebbe duck out the other door a time or two and take a few shots at 'em. I'd jest as soon they didn't see me headin' thet way, 'cause Esperanza's still in the house. Leastways, I figger she must be. She wasn't out there when they were fixin' to hang you, *compadre*."

Solamon overheard what I'd said. "Miss Esperanza isn't in the house, McCowan. She and that other lady left early this morning with Captain Conover and a squad of troopers. She didn't want to leave, but he forced her to go. Told her she'd be better off in town, where she couldn't get mixed up in what might be happening here."

I grabbed him by the arm. "When did they leave, man? It must've been before daylight, 'cause that's when they rousted us out. What town was he talkin' about? Juno? Ain't no hotel there, jest Miz Sawyer's lodgin' house, and thet's not no fit place for a lady to stay. What's thet sidewinder up to, you reckon? Surely he knows what happens to a man out here if he brings harm to a woman. The orneriest galoot in the western lands would think twice before he'd do anything bad to a lady. I wonder if Gresham knows what he's done. I believe I'll jest ask him right now.''

He was lying on his side in a corner, his hands tied behind his back. His eyes grew bigger'n saucers when he seen me heading his way, and he started squirming.

"Don't you dare touch me, you oversized moron!" he cried out. "I have friends in high places, and you'll pay dearly for this. You'll see. You're still in hot water, and Dills will break in here any minute now.''

"I wouldn't dirty my hands on you," I told him. "I would have killed you a long time ago, but I'd sooner see you beg for mercy when they put the rope around your neck. Now, we need some answers from you, and I mean to have them, or thet hangman's gonna be hard put to find a place for the rope.

"Where is the captain plannin' to take Esperanza, and why did you let her leave the ranch? You'd better tell me, or I might jest carve off some of your belly fat. Talk! Now!''

He stared up at me, bewildered by what I'd just told him. "Why . . . why . . . I have no idea! He *took* Esperanza, you say?'' Puzzled, he struggled to find words. "I can't imagine why he would do a thing like that. Honestly. He didn't take her away with *my* permission. You may be sure of that.'' Shaking his head in wonderment, he muttered half to himself, "I can't believe he would do anything so foolish. I could see that he was infatuated with her, but to spirit her away . . .''

Disgusted, I walked away and went to where Carlos sat in his chair. I told him what Solamon had said to me, and he was alarmed. "You must go after them," he told me. "She is in great danger. My daughter would rather die than submit, and she will kill herself if he attempts to molest her. We cannot take any chances, Lysander. You must leave, and now. Somehow you must break through and catch up with them.''

I was sick at heart, but I knew this wasn't possible. We had to have the ammunition first, or he and all the others would be killed. I explained that Esperanza had a gun, that she would use it if she had to, and that I couldn't believe the captain would use force.

"He's been moonin' over her like a sick calf," I assured him. "He ain't about to do her no harm. Only thing that'll be hurt is his feelin's. You can tell—he thinks he's some kind of Don Juan, and I reckon he figgers ain't no woman can turn him down. All he'll offer is marriage. Soon's we take care of our problem here, I'll take out after them. In the meantime she'll be safe enough, so don't you worry none."

Against his protests, I got ready to make my move. The gunfire from Dills's bunch had increased, and looking out the window, I could see they'd taken over both bunkhouses. Some were up on the roofs, where the parapets gave them cover. A distraction of some kind was what I needed, but I couldn't think of anything that didn't mean using up what few rounds of ammunition we had remaining. Then it struck me.

The horses! If I could get the corral gate open without getting myself shot, then I'd stampede the whole herd right into Dills's position. In the confusion, I should be able to run to the house and enter the secret room. Coming back to the barn might be another story, but at least I'd have guns, and plenty of ammunition for them.

I told Mr. Gilkie and Vargas what I planned to try, and they agreed it was worth doing. Mr. Gilkie insisted on giving me his LeMat, just in case I ran into some scout out of Dills's outfit. "You go on and take it," he told me. "We've no need for the gun here, because it's only good for close-up shootin'. It's loaded to the hilt, includin' thet bottom barrel, but I ain't got no more powder to spare." He showed me how to move the hammer nose up and down so's to shoot a round from either the cylinder or the buckshot barrel.

"You take care now, y'hear me! Don't you go lookin' for trouble or doin' nothin' foolish. Jest git in there, latch on to them guns and ca'tridges, and hustle on back down here. I'm gonna sneak out in back and help you hoorah them horses outta thet corral. You jest git thet gate open and I'll do the rest. G'wan, now! You give me an owl hoot when you're ready to open thet gate. Good luck, son."

Slinging the LeMat over my shoulder, I moved to the door. Luckily, some of the horses were right up against the poles and crowding each other. I got down on my knees and slipped under the bottom rail. Keeping low, I crawled along, the horses sidestepping to avoid trampling me. The worst part came when I reached the corner post and a big sorrel stud decided I was intruding on his territory.

He reared and came down on his forefeet, narrowly missed my head, and tried again. This time I dodged his feet and, reaching behind his left foreleg, grabbed his right just above the ankle. Squeezing the cannon bones, I threw my left shoulder against him and pulled hard on his leg, dropping him heavily on his side. While he was squealing and trying to figger out what had happened I scuttled to the gate.

Cupping my hand, I sounded the hoot of a barn owl, softly repeating it twice. In answer I heard the *creee creee* of the red-tailed hawk and threw the gate open as the old man started whooping and hollering at those horses.

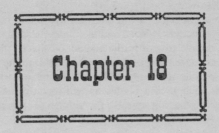

Chapter 18

Rush McCowan was bone-tired, and white alkali grit caked his sweat-soaked shirt and ringed his eyes and mouth. The scraggly, broom-tailed pony he rode was diminutive, so small his spur rowels dragged the ground at times as he approached the outskirts of Juno. Nine hundred miles of hard riding lay behind him, and he'd covered that distance in a week—a week of hardly pausing except to catnap, feed and water his horses, and gulp down a few mouthfuls of whatever was handy.

At twenty-seven, the eldest of the three brothers, the week on the trail had pared twenty pounds off his normal two-twenty and left him looking older and meaner. Black slanted eyes squinted from under shelves of protruding bone, and his high cheekbones, a gift from his Indian father, shone starkly on his copper-hued face. Deep crescent lines bordered a wide generous mouth. Lines that weren't nearly so apparent only a week before. He rode loosely, slumped shoulders moving in cadence with the pony's running walk, and long legs dangling straight, in the Indian way.

On a lead rope was a big chestnut horse that staggered on failing legs. Its eyes, glazed and lackluster, stared without seeing at the double row of frame and adobe shacks that lined the town's main street. Beside him was the twin to the pony Rush was riding, this one carrying Rush's roundup bed and camp gear. Both were Kiowa ponies he had traded for on the trail. Hardy little beasts, but scarcely big enough for a man of Rush's size.

He'd left Fort Kearny, in the year-old state of Nebraska, with the girl he loved lying wounded in the post hospital and justified anger in his heart. Rode out with no time to say goodbye or explain why he had to leave. Rode out with the fort's commander standing, incredulous, on the headquarters porch, the telegram flimsy in his hand. "I'll do the best I can," the officer had shouted. "I'll explain, but I doubt that she'll understand, McCowan, or ever forgive you."

How could she understand? Rush asked himself. Who could, or would, understand why he'd ridden away, leaving her hurt and unconscious and alone? He loved her. He'd told her he loved her, and she had said she loved him too. They'd made plans. Talked about going to Omaha City, and mebbe even to Chicago. Of marrying and building a life together. Of restoring the stage line she owned, and working side by side to make it a success. Now all that was down the drain.

The telegraphed message from his mother had been explicit in wording, and he'd had no other choice:

COME HOME NOW. CARLOS AND LYSANDER BAD HURT. SOME MEN DEAD. SAME LIKE WAR. NEED YOUR HELP. NO WANT LOSE MILO. ABIGAIL MCCOWAN, CAMP HUDSON.

Maybe Ada *would* understand, and forgive him. After all,

she'd seen her father killed by greedy men, and she believed in strong family ties. He shook his head. Time would tell, and he had other, bigger problems facing him, and they couldn't wait. He needed rest, but even more, he had to see to his animals' needs, and that must come first.

The stage company maintained a large barn, and it was toward this barn that Rush guided the pony. Just inside the double doors a small boy with a mop of black hair stared in wonder at the strange-looking cavalcade.

"You work here, boy?" Rush's voice rasped hoarsely, and the boy jumped fearfully.

"Yessir," he piped back. "Whatcher got in mind?"

A silver dollar appeared in Rush's hand, and he tossed it to the lad. Climbing down wearily from the little pony, he handed over the reins.

"Unsaddle this scrub, and take the pack off of the other, then give 'em a bait of hay and turn 'em out in the corral. Now listen carefully, boy. I want partic'lar attention for this here chestnut horse, you hear? You wipe him off with a bit of wet sackin', then let him have jest a mite of water to drink. Not much—jest enough to wet his whistle. Then a couple quarts of oats, and you rub him down good with some dry sackin'. Once he's cooled down real good, you take and put him in a clean stall with plenty of beddin'. Somewhere in this barn you must have a clean dry blanket, and I want you to put it over him and make sure it stays on. Last, go up there in the loft and find some hay with plenty of good leaf, and you feed it to him. Carefully, now. Don't you go to founderin' him, or I'll skin you alive. You hear me?"

Wide-eyed, the boy could only stand there and nod. "You can count on me, mister," he finally managed to blurt out.

"All right, then," Rush growled. "You do a good job and there's another dollar in it for you. I'll be over to thet saloon. When I come back I want to see my saddle on a good horse. The best you've got. You understand?" Again, a nod was all the boy could manage for a moment, then he spoke up to his fearsome-looking customer with his shoulders squared.

"This ain't no livery barn, mister. I'll do like I said and tend to your critters, but I can't lend you no horse. I ain't apologiz-in'—I'm tellin' you. Them's the rules.''

To the boy's amazement the man's face softened, and when he spoke it was in a gentler tone. ''I admire your spunk, boy. Ain't many, your age or older, would turn me down the way you just done. I'll tell you what—if your boss says anythin', then you jest tell him thet Rush McCowan asked for thet horse, and he'll understand. Is thet all right?''

The boy's eyes grew round in wonder. ''Are you really truly *the* Rush McCowan?'' he shrilled. ''Gosh A'mighty! Don't thet beat all? Rush McCowan! Wait'll I tell my friend! He ain't gonna b'lieve me!''

He leaned forward and whispered, ''You here to take keer of them fellers thet's got all of your folks tied up somewhere's?'' Looking around, he stared up at Rush. ''Where at's the rest of your bunch? You ain't gonna take 'em all on alone, are yuh? Must be at least a coupla hun'ert of 'em. Honest to Betsy, Rush, er, uh, *Mister* McCowan. I never b'lieved for a minute thet none of your folks was plannin' to do nothin' wrong. No matter what them fellers told my pap.''

Rush grinned down at the boy. ''Thanks for sayin' thet, sonny. By the way, what's your name? You sound like the kind of man I'll want to remember.''

The boy flushed. ''Name's Stuart,'' he said. ''Bennet C. Stuart, same's my pap, and his before him. I'll git a horse ready for yuh, Mr. McCowan. We got us a dandy in a back stall. He's a big horse, too. Mebbe even big enough for a big feller like you. The boss don't ride him much, 'cause he's sorta skeered of him, but I figger you can handle most any horse, no matter how bad he might be. You jest have you a drink or two, and he'll be waitin' right here.'' Squaring his thin shoulders again, the boy led the chestnut into the depths of the barn, the two Indian po-nies following behind.

Mindful of the dust and dirt he'd accumulated on the way down, Rush caught up with Ben Stuart. ''I forgot thet I'll need some things outta my saddlebags,'' he told him. ''And it might be a good idea to take along my rifle,'' he added. The worn, scarred buttstock of a Henry showed in his scabbard, a fine, engraved rifle he'd traded for in the Nations. With it in one hand, he rummaged in a saddlebag and got all that he needed out of a pocket. "See you later, Ben," he said.

Out in back, Rush took off his shirt and ducked head and shoulders into the horse tank, scrubbing vigorously with his hands at his face and hair, then drying on one of the towels that hung nearby. He'd taken a clean shirt from his saddlebags, which he now donned, taking off his gunbelt to tuck in the shirttails. With his hat, he brushed dust off his pants legs as best he could, and strapped the gunbelt back around his waist. Combing his hair with his fingers, he put on the hat and walked back through the barn, stopping to stuff his dirty shirt in a pocket of his saddlebags, then pointing his steps in the direction of Dutchy's Saloon.

Pausing to look over the batwing doors, he saw that there was only one customer at the bar, a man about his own age who looked strangely familiar. Entering the room, he walked over to the bar and ordered a beer.

The bartender turned around and a smile spread from ear to ear as he thrust out his hand. "Rush McCowan!" he exclaimed. "As I live and breathe, it's really you! I about gave up ever seeing you again. You remember me, don't you? I'm Franz Osterhouse, Dutchy's nephew. I rode trail for you last year, when we took the herds to Abilene." As his smile slowly faded, his face took on a more somber cast.

"I suppose you've come about the trouble," he said. "The soldiers that have taken over your folks' place. I'm sorry about that, Rush. There's been lots of stories, and most of the people hereabouts believe them, so nobody's lifted one finger to help out. There's a few of the old gang who talk about getting up a bunch to go out there, but so far it's a lot of talk and nothing else."

The stranger at the bar, a tall man in a black suit, with long black hair hanging below his shirt collar, turned and smiled, showing even white teeth. "May I join you in what I call my toast to fair-weather friends?" he asked. Holding his mug of beer aloft, still smiling, he recited:

"Here's to mine, them as treats me fine,
So fine you'd never know,
That when I'm down, they're not around,
And all their talk's just blow."

He tipped up his mug and drank deeply, then thrust out a hand. "I'm Mahlon. Your cousin Mahlon McCowan, and here to back you up with my guns, if you'll have me. Let me warn you, however. I've found out the hard way that a man who's following the rules doesn't always come out on top. I know Texans have strong ideals about giving the other man an even break, and fighting fair. *Fairness* is not one of my strong points. If this bothers you, then I'll go alone." He swung open his coat and showed Rush two ten-gauge shotguns that hung, one under each arm, with a thong. Both buttstocks had been sawn off, leaving just the pistol grip, with a hole for the thong, and the barrels cut back to about fifteen inches.

"Never was much of a hand with pistols," he said. "So I took to using beauties like these." He grasped one by its grip and brought it up level. The gaping maws yawned at Rush, and instinctively he stepped back a pace.

A thin chuckle came from over near the door, and both men swung around after setting their drinks on the bar.

A long, lean man clad in greasy buckskins stood tall in the doorway, a short-barreled carbine hanging from his right hand, and two Colt revolvers holstered on a belt around his waist. Still chuckling, he allowed the doors to swing closed behind him and moved toward them, the carbine's muzzle pointed at the floor. Black stubble covered his cheeks, and a huge black mustache swept down over the corners of a wide mouth, almost to his square-cut chin. The tip of an ear was missing, and several white scars were vivid on his bronzed face. He grinned and transferred the carbine to his other hand. "You must be Rush McCowan," he said. "I'm brother to thet ugly galoot standin' there next to you." He stuck out his hand and grasped Rush's in a firm clasp. "Me? I'm Cassius Marcellus McCowan," he said. "The old man must have been readin' Roman history when he stuck thet handle on me. Most folks call me Cass, and

I'm pleased to see you, cousin. We seen each other once, back in Kentucky, a long time ago."

Rush nodded. "I remember now. Thet's why your brother looked familiar when I first seen him at the bar. Back mebbe fifteen years ago your pa come to visit and brought you with him. We were jest younkers then. Real surprise, seein' you here in Juno. What brings you to the Val Verde? You huntin' a place to settle down in your old age?"

"Nosir, I ain't. Can't afford to." He smiled. "I'm a wanted man, Rush. There's folks in prac'ly every place you could name thet's jest itchin' to git their paws on me.

"S'funny, how a man can git hisself into trouble so durn easy. Started with me havin' to shoot a feller 'cause his dander was up and he was bound he was gonna kill me. Next thing you knowed there was his cousin, and I barely missed gittin' kilt thet time." He fingered the ragged tip of his ear. "It was him thet almost bit off this ear. Hadn't've been for him bein' so cocky, and thinkin' he had me cold, we wouldn't be standin' here talkin'. Leastways, I wouldn't.

"After that, it was catch as catch can. Either an old-timey gunfighter wantin' to show he could still cut the mustard, or some two-bit youngster figgerin' to build up a big name for hisself. Like I said, there's posters out on me, but I ain't never really crossed the line. Oh, sure! I put my brand on a stray calf or two, like most everybody, but I ain't never robbed nobody." He frowned.

"I was passin' through Barlow's Ferry, on the Nueces, and the storekeep there recognized me. Bein' a lonesome cuss, he wanted to gab, but I was sorta in a hurry. Jest as I was pullin' out, he told me about the trouble here. Acted like mebbe he figgered thet'd make me ask more questions. Well, I did! Jest enough to know I'd best git on over here. So here I am, ready to help out. Where do we start, cousin?"

Mahlon spoke up. "Bad news sure travels fast, don't it, fellers? Me, I was clear down in Port Isabel when I got the word. Right now I'm ready to start evening the odds."

Young Osterhouse had gone to the far end of the bar, wiping industriously with a wet cloth, obviously trying to be inconspicuous. Crooking a finger, Rush called for another round of beers. As the youngster set the mugs in front of them, Rush asked what he'd meant by stories, and why people had believed them. "Us McCowans ain't never done no harm to any of the folks around here," he told him.

Osterhouse fidgeted, and his face reddened. "Why, it's not my place to repeat 'em, Rush. I really don't know just what-all's been said. Something about Don Carlos planning a big takeover with Milo and Lysander. According to what I heard from the soldiers, they were planning to make everyone in the valley just give up their places and move on. This land commissioner from back in Washington found out they'd filed on every water hole in the Val Verde and were claiming to own all the land around them. He had copies of their filings—the commissioner, that is. That's all I know. The folks were pretty mad at first. There was talk of lynching Don Carlos, along with your brothers, but the colonel—the boss of those soldiers—he said they were here to make sure we wouldn't lose our land. That the culprits—that's his word, not mine—would be punished." He shrugged. "I'd tell you more, Rush, if I could, but that's all I know."

Rush's face darkened. His deep-set eyes glinted as a bulge appeared on his jawline. Carefully he set his mug down on the bar and wiped his hands on his pants legs.

"Let's go," he said quietly. "I gotta pick up my horse over to the stage company barn. I'll meet you fellers right out front in five minutes." Turning, he walked toward the door. One hand on the batwings, he stopped and turned to face them. "I'd better not see you outta this saloon, young feller. Leastways, not while I'm still in town. I wouldn't take it kindly was you to tell folks about us bein' here."

The doors swung to behind him, leaving one badly shaken barkeep wiping his brow. "Rush oughta know better'n that," he said. "Why, I owe him a lot! Hadn't been for him allowing me and my brother along on last year's drive, I'd just be working for my uncle, instead of owning a half interest."

Mahlon grinned, but there was no humor in his eyes. "I suggest you start remembering that, friend. If you just got to run off at the mouth, see if you can find something nice to say about the McCowans. Let's move on out, Cass. Air is a little fresher over by the horse barn.''

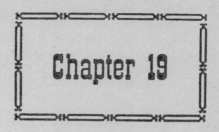

Chapter 19

Captain Frank Conover was pleased with himself, and as he thought back over the past twenty-four hours, he wished his arms were long enough so he could pat himself on the back. Gresham was stupid. No matter how many papers he forced the two prisoners to sign, his claims would never be valid. No, the federal court would soon discover the truth and appoint a genuine commissioner to ferret out the facts. The crooked schemer would be thrown off the rancho and likely land in a federal prison. He'd be lucky if he got only twenty years.

His was the only way that made any sense. Marry the don's daughter, and control the land through his wife. The girl was reluctant right now, but she'd soon change her attitude once he had her alone. Imagine! A real beauty, and still an old maid at twenty-six! Damned strange that some of these country bumpkins hadn't tried to pay her court. It could be that she really didn't like men at all. He'd had occasion to read about such women. Well, she'd soon have a chance to find out differently. As his wife, there'd be no such foolishness in the privacy of their bedroom.

Still, she had shown a certain fondness for that oversized cowboy, McCowan. Literally went without sleep so he could have proper care for his wounds. Hmmm . . . I wonder if perhaps there wasn't a little hanky-panky going on while we assumed he was gravely ill and perhaps even dying?

Esperanza reined in and dropped back beside his bay. A frown on her face, she asked where he was taking her. "We cannot stay in Juno," she said. "After all, there isn't any accommodation there except for a very questionable boardinghouse that caters only to unmarried men. I demand to know why you've spirited Señora Honrada and me away from the rancho in the middle of the night. Just what do you intend to accomplish by this, Captain?"

Conover smiled. "All in good time, dear lady. All in good time. Meanwhile, isn't it a beautiful day to be out in the open? The sun is shi—" He stood in his stirrups and shaded his eyes, peering ahead. Three riders had topped a rise in the road and were closing with them fast.

"Sergeant! Take two men and find out who they are. The other three troopers will stay here with us. Double-time, man! What's the matter? Why aren't you following my order? I'll have those stripes if you don't move out now!"

The unhappy sergeant was shaking his head. "I'm sorry, Captain. I ain't too sure we're supposed to be out here on this road, escorting these two ladies. You wouldn't let me check with the colonel, and I don't know what he's gonna say about this. I do know that Southerners, and Texans in particular, are mighty mean when you go to fooling with one of their women. As second-in-command, I would suggest that our best course is to stay together until we know who they are. After all, we have them outnumbered, sir."

He ordered a halt, in spite of the captain's protests. A loose skirmish line was formed by the six troopers, flanking the captain and the women. "You there, Thompson," the sergeant barked. "Wipe that scared look off your face!"

They waited as the three riders approached, seemingly in no great hurry as they trotted their horses. Esperanza's heart leaped as she recognized Rush McCowan riding between the other two men, who were complete strangers to her.

Rush swept his hat off his head and bowed slightly. He straightened in the saddle, a big smile on his face. "Howdy do, ladies. You too, Cap'n. Sure is a nice day! Where-at might you be headin'? Camp Hudson's over that-a-way, on San Pedro Creek, and Fort Davis is clean over the mountains—must be three hundred miles. Ain't no other Army camps near here thet I know of. You folks ain't lost, are you?"

Conover eyed him suspiciously. He noted they were all well armed and well mounted. Definitely not just ordinary ranch hands, he decided. Perhaps better to speak politely. After all, it made no sense for them to involve themselves in a petty disagreement with these men when he had such an important and critical mission to conclude. Better to address them as equals and take no chances of an altercation erupting that could easily result in one of his party being injured.

"These ladies are citizens of Mexico," he said. "My men and I are escorting them to the border, where they will meet with their families. I thank you men for your concern. However, I assure you that we are not lost, and we *are* in somewhat of a hurry. We bid you good day, sir. Come, Sergeant. Let's get this column moving. We don't want to be forced to pitch camp, you know." Kneeing the bay, he rode between two of the riders and spurred into an easy lope, waving for the others to follow him.

Grinning at Esperanza, Rush gigged his horse between her and the escort, forcing her mount and that of her friend to shy and move back, safely away from the others.

"*Heeee! Haaaah!!* Take 'em, boys! Thet cap'n's all mine! You take care of them others whilst I run him down." Rush, his rebel yell still echoing across the prairie, whirled his horse around, hoofs pawing the air, and raked his spurs into the animal's flanks.

Conover was astounded. Suddenly his whole world tumbled down like a house of cards. His men were scattering, and a madman was bearing down on him like a hungry beast, screaming some hideous battle cry and brandishing a revolver. He heard the resounding boom of a shotgun and saw two troopers swept from their saddles. Another tumbled to the ground as a rifle cracked, and the rest were riding for their lives.

Terrified, he reined the bay around and spurred it savagely, with only one thing in his mind—to get as far away as he possibly could. There wasn't any way he could make it back to the rancho. Too far. But the town was no more than three or four miles. If he could reach Juno, he might find someone to help him. Forgotten was the land, and his grandiose scheme for wealth and power. Forgotten was his lust for the girl, and his plans to break her spirit. All of his efforts now must be concentrated on just saving his life.

When Rush had hollered his rebel yell, Cass wasted a shot after the fleeing captain. Rush's claim on the man came in time to make Cass deliberately miss. After all, he wouldn't want to spoil his cousin's fun, would he? Swinging back for another target, he felt a bullet sear his shoulder, and shot back at the sergeant, who was bringing his rifle up for another try. The other troopers were having trouble controlling their horses, and their shooting was erratic.

Mahlon swung up one of his shotguns and emptied two saddles, the troopers literally blown off their mounts. One of the others panicked, the trooper named Thompson, throwing his rifle to one side and screaming, "Don't shoot! God! Don't kill me! I'll—" A slug from Cass's carbine knocked him out of the saddle, and he fell to the ground. Mahlon, in pursuit of another man, brought his second gun level and blew the trooper's head from his shoulders. For a few more strides the body stayed erect, then toppled off.

A scream from Esperanza stopped Mahlon in his tracks. A

wounded trooper hopping on his good leg had caught hold of her arm and was trying to drag her from the horse. His own mount lay dead on the ground. Afraid to shoot for fear of hitting the girl, Mahlon spurred his horse, trying hard to reach her in time. Halfway there, he saw Esperanza point to the man with something small in her hand. A puff of white smoke blossomed around her fist. Mahlon heard a faint crack, and the man fell backwards, cluthing at his face.

Reining up, Mahlon watched as Esperanza wiped tears from her cheeks with her sleeve. Groping into the pocket of her dress, she brought out a small cartridge and fitted it into the derringer she held in her other hand. "I think I killed him," she said quietly. "I had no other choice."

Stepping down, Mahlon rolled the man over with his boot.

"Yep," he told her. "You sure enough killed him, all right. Nailed him right square between the eyes. He didn't expect it, and he never knew what hit him. You did good, girl!"

Looking down at him, she shuddered. "How can you be so callous?" she asked. "I just took a man's life, but I never meant it to happen. Doesn't life mean anything to you? I'm aware that you can argue I shot this man to protect myself, but that isn't really true. He wasn't trying to harm me; he was just frightened and needed my horse." She looked away, and her shoulders began to shake.

Mahlon studied her for a moment. Then, choosing his words carefully, he spoke. "You've just killed a man. That's a true fact, and there isn't any way you can undo what happened. More important is to regard it for what it really was—a thing that you had to do or get yourself hurt. Right now it might be a good idea to comfort your friend. She appears to be mighty upset, and she's crying her eyes out."

Esperanza put the derringer in her pocket and dismounted from her horse. "She'll stop crying when she's ready. I just realized that you've been wounded, and that's something I *can* remedy. Take off your trousers, please."

Mahlon stared at her, mouth agape. Then, looking down, he saw a spreading red stain on his right thigh. "Well, if that don't beat all! Would you believe, I never felt a darn thing. But I do now!'' He began backing away. "It's just a crease, ma'am, honest! Another quarter inch and it would have missed me completely." He held up his hands. "It's not worth fooling with, ma'am. It'll heal all by itself."

Lifting her hem, Esperanza tore off a strip of petticoat. "This was freshly laundered just yesterday. I'd rather use a regular bandage, but this will do. Please . . . Why, I just realized, I don't even know who you are!''

"My name is Mahlon McCowan, ma'am. Rush is a cousin, and that other fellow, wherever he's got to, is my brother. You see, my father is Abigail McCowan's brother." He bowed.

Rolling up the strip of muslin, she smiled. "Esperanza Montoncillo, señor, and I'm happy to make your acquaintance. We've met under somewhat unusual circumstances, have we not? Now, let's see what can be done about your leg. Remove your trousers—or shall I do it for you?'' Against his protests, she made him drop his pants, enough so she could clean and bandage the wounded leg.

A mile away, the one-sided battle was almost over. Cass, his right shoulder bloodied by a bullet from the sergeant's rifle, cornered his man at the foot of a bluff. Not able to force his horse up the steep bank, the sergeant swung around in his saddle and worked the lever of his rifle. The empty that fell on the ground was from his last cartridge. He sat there defiantly clutching at the pommel.

"Go ahead, you bloody murderer!'' he cried. "What are you waiting for? Shoot, damn you, shoot!'' He'd been shot twice through the body, and one leg was broken by a bullet. Barely able to stay in the saddle, he stared at Cass. The tears came unbidden to his eyes as he cried out in frustration, "Kill me, you murderous devil! What's holding you back?''

Cass shoved his rifle in its scabbard and rode forward. "I ain't gonna shoot you, mister. You're a brave man, and I can't shoot you down like a helpless critter. C'mon! I'll take you back to where them women are, and mebbe they can do somethin' about thet bleedin'.''

* * *

The captain's bay and Rush's borrowed mount were similar in build and stamina. It had become a race, with Conover a few hundred yards in the lead and Rush reluctant to use his guns. Knowing the officer must be a key man in the hoax, he wanted to bring him down and find out some answers. Twice Conover had turned in the saddle and fired back at Rush, an elusive target on the galloping horse. Each time he'd had to slow somewhat, and the distance between them had narrowed, but he was still far in the lead.

Now Juno was not much more than a mile ahead, and Rush's chances of stopping him were diminishing. If Conover wasn't stopped before he reached the town, Rush would have to turn back. With most of the townsfolk believing the stories, the captain would find many supporters, and they'd protect him.

He hated to do it, but there was only one way to stop the man. Shoot his horse. Gauging the distance between them to be roughly two hundred yards, Rush pulled the Henry from the scabbard. Taking the reins in his teeth, he lifted the leaf sight and peered at the tiny numbers. With the bouncing, it was difficult to do, but he managed to set the bar at the correct range. It would be a tough shot to make, but he had to try. His horse was laboring, but his stride was evenly paced and could be calculated.

Standing in the stirrups, Rush brought up the rifle, centering the front sight in the bar's notch. Aiming below the root of the horse's tail, he took in a deep breath, let part of it out, and squeezed the trigger.

The resulting cloud of dirty white smoke hid the target until Rush rode through it and saw that the horse was down and Conover was getting to his feet. As Rush thundered down on him, the officer was fumbling at his holster, but his gun was gone. His face ashen, he knelt and tried to pull out a carbine that was pinned under the fallen animal, but it was held tight by the weight of the dead horse.

Rush drew up a few feet away and stepped down. Shoving the Henry back in its scabbard, he turned around and faced Conover, who was staring, wild-eyed, like a trapped animal.

"Your string's run out," he told him. "Now, I want a few

answers to some mighty important questions, and you're gonna tell me everythin' you know. If you don't, I'm gonna make a believer out of you. I'm normally a peaceable man, but this batch of lies you've been tellin' about my family has me a mite upset. Matter of fact, I'm madder'n an old, sore-toothed mama grizzly, so I aim to do somethin' about you, and right now.'' Unbuckling his gunbelt, he hung it on the saddle horn and turned around, doubling his big fists.

Advancing on Conover, he warned him, ''You'd best start talkin', hombre, and you can begin by tellin' me what you'd planned for Esperanza, 'cause she's a very special friend of mine. You lied about takin' her to the border. She's not a Mexican citizen, and her family's right here in Texas.

''Then there's this business about takin' over our place, and doin' the same at Rancho Montoncillo. My maw tells me thet my baby brother and Don Carlos have been hurt by your men. How bad, I don't know yet, but you're gonna pay dearly; you can bet your boots on thet. Stand still, durn you!''

Conover had been steadily retreating as Rush came toward him, until they were some distance from Rush's horse. Looking suddenly confident, Conover stopped and drew his saber with a ringing metallic clang. ''Now,'' he jeered, ''let's see if your size will protect you from this!'' Lunging forward, he swung it in a mighty slash aimed at Rush's head; had it connected, it would have ended the encounter.

Ducking barely in time, Rush stumbled and fell. With a triumphant scream, Conover lifted the blade high in the air with both hands and struck downward as Rush rolled away in desperation, scrabbling on hands and knees, trying to escape the slashing blade.

Back on his feet, Rush circled warily. Supremely confident, the captain acted now as if he were instructing in the art of swordsmanship. Flourishing the heavy saber, he advanced a step toward Rush and lunged, cutting at the air with a slashing motion, all the while reciting in a monotonous, toneless voice exactly what he was doing and why. It seemed to have become a game with him, and Rush was suddenly aware that the captain was now insane. Somehow, whether it was either the enormity of the monstrous hoax or something else that had affected him, he had lost touch with reality and was a dangerous maniac.

Seeing a length of thick mesquite root in the sand, Rush grabbed it in time to parry another vicious slash. Looking behind him, he saw the edge of a shallow arroyo and thought this might be his only chance. Stumbling back, he faked a fall, and as Conover rushed forward, raising the sword, Rush planted his feet in the madman's belly, grabbed at his hand, and catapulted the man over his head. A heavy thump and an agonized shriek were followed by a thrashing sound and pebbles rattling against larger stones. Then silence.

Shakily, Rush got to his feet and leaned over for a moment, his hands on his knees. His heart was pounding like it was about to jump out of his chest. Then he straightened up and went to the edge of the arroyo.

Captain Conover lay facedown with half the length of the saber's blade protruding from his back. He wasn't moving. Stumbling down into the shallow wash, Rush attempted to turn the body over but couldn't. Looking close, he realized the hilt of the sword was lodged between two large rocks, which held it securely. He'd have to lift the body off the blade in order to move it.

For a moment, he thought of just letting the captain lie there, but there was a possibility he was carrying documents, something that might help prove the conspiracy, so he decided to unskewer the body, so to speak, and search the clothing. A tough, messy job, but no problem for Rush, since Conover had been a thin, lightly built man.

Laying the body down, he rummaged through the uniform. A back pants pocket yielded a wallet with about two hundred dollars in Yankee currency and a *carte de visite* photo of an older, thin-faced woman, perhaps Conover's mother.

An inside pocket of the short shell jacket contained two envelopes. One was a letter postmarked Gallatin, Missouri. A quick glance showed it to be from some woman, and the last paragraph was a plea for money. The other envelope had what appeared to be orders from Washington assigning Conover the command in the Reconstruction Army. With it was a note in which someone named Silas P. Gresham outlined the plan for confiscating property in western Texas. It promised Conover a large share of the profits when the ranches were sold. A line warned him not to allow more than a cursory look at his orders, since they were forgeries. Well, if that wasn't the evidence he needed, then nothing was. All he had to do was show them to the authorities at Fort Davis and all of those lying stories going around would be scotched for good.

Pocketing the letters and the wallet, he decided to keep the captain's saber. Like the guns that he and Milo had picked up on various battlefields during the war, it would be sort of a memento of what had happened. He reached down and unbuckled the belt and scabbard and laid them aside. Just a few minutes' work served to tumble down the bank of the narrow wash and cover the body. Then he gathered a few rocks and placed them on top. This would discourage foraging animals and prevent them from uncovering the corpse.

Then, sheathing the saber, he walked back to where he had left his horse. Strapping the gunbelt around his waist and mounting up, he rode to rejoin the others. They were about to pull out when he arrived, and Mahlon explained, after he told them about the captain falling on his sword.

"The sergeant tells us we'd best hurry," Mahlon told him. "When he 'n' his bunch left, early this morning, he heard some talk about stringing up Lysander and Esperanza's pa. Said the boss of the bunch wanted them to sign off on their land, and if they refused, he'd hang 'em one at a time. Now, the three of us ain't gonna be enough to whip the whole bunch; I know that. The sergeant says they got about a hundred men. But still, I figger we ought to try, don't you?"

The sergeant's leg had been splinted, and his wounds and the slight ones suffered by Cass and Mahlon were all treated. Rush hadn't gotten a scratch, and considered himself to be lucky. The sergeant insisted he was able to stay up on a horse, so they boosted him into the saddle.

"I'd like to be able to bury the others," he said, "but I reckon that can be done later. Right now, we'd better hurry up and get back to that ranch if you men plan to save your friends from hanging. Even now we may be too late."

Epilogue

Wellsir, there's no need to let you know that we came out on top, 'cause if we'd lost, then I'd never be sitting here and telling you folks this story, would I?

Let's see now, where'd I leave off? Oh, yeah! We had the horses stampeding out of the corral, and me running with 'em so's I could get into the house and bring back a bunch of ammunition. I made it slicker'n grease and was about a step away from the door to that secret room when I heard me a big commotion in the front entry.

The doors busted open, and who's a-standing there bigger'n life but my brother Milo McCowan. Alongside of him were cousin Trace, and my pa's brother, Uncle Handsome Horse.

They taken me out in front, where I seen mebbe fifty men, all armed to the teeth. They even had one of the rapid-fire guns that old man Gatling built up. I recognized most, but there were about twenty big Injuns I'd never seen before.

Old Eli Sprague was there, of course, and the two Kiowas, Pak and Tunk, that we'd sorta adopted into our family. Some of the boys we'd taken along to Abilene a year before were in that crowd, together with some neighbors we knew no more than to say howdy do if they was to ride by. Still, they had belted on their six-guns, picked up their rifles, and done what they figgered was right and proper for neighbors.

I told Milo how things stood inside, and he just gave me one of them big grins of his. Told me not to worry myself, that he'd take care of everything and everybody.

That was when I noticed that there was more'n just a few friends camped out there. Behind them there must've been a half a hundred men wearing blue uniforms and sitting there with their hands tied. Milo walked over to one who had the bars of a captain on his shoulders. He untied the feller's hands and talked with him a minute or so.

The captain kept nodding, and looking around at all them armed men, and nodding some more. Once he looked sorta unhappy, but he nodded again. Finally he'n Milo shook hands with each other, and they walked into the house. I moved to follow along, but Milo waved me back with another grin. We watched as they disappeared into that house.

Whilst we were waiting I talked with Handsome Horse, and he introduced me to two more cousins of mine—Hone McCowan and his brother, Hutch, who'd been cowboying down south and were about my same age, I'd guess.

Milo and the captain were still inside those walls when we heard the sounds of running horses and I got me another big surprise. My big brother Rush came galloping in with Esperanza, that other lady, and three fellers I'd never seen before. One of 'em had on a uniform, and he looked about to fall off his horse: he was that bad hurt.

I ran on over to Rush, and he wrapped his arms around me and looked up, something he didn't have to do very often, I guess. We made a fuss over each other, and then I was helping my Esperanza down off her horse, and she kissed me about forty-'leven times, with me kissing her back. All them fellers was a-laughing and a-hooting, but me 'n' her couldn't have cared less. I was so darned glad to see her safe, the whole world could've been watching and it wouldn't have mattered none. In between kisses we told Rush of our plan to marry, and the sooner the better.

We helped get that sergeant down and over to some shade. Somebody brought over a canteen and gave him a drink. Rush explained about him, and introduced Mahlon and Cass. There wasn't anybody hadn't heard about Cass McCowan, 'cause them posters must have decorated just about every fence post and tree between here and the Canadian line. He walked over a ways and looked over all those prisoners sitting there looking real glum. One of them, of course, was Len Chidden, the deputy U.S. marshal who'd bragged he'd run him down if it taken him a month of Sundays. Right now he looked beaten. He just hung his head and had nothing to say.

After everybody quieted down, Rush asked me how I come to have this scar running down the side of my face. You know, I'd forgotten it was there. So much had been going on that I hadn't had time to think about it. So I told him part of what'd taken place—how I'd gone a little crazy when I saw Carlos wounded and Poco Luce lying dead on the floor. He nodded, saddened by the news about Poco Luce, then went over to his horse and taken that saber from the saddle horn. The next thing I knowed, he was handing me the sword and telling me it was mine to keep. We still have it. I reckon you saw it. It's hanging over the fireplace in the parlor.

About then, Milo came to the doors, and Miguel Vargas was with him. They told us that Dills had decided to surrender and take his chances with the law. Carlos wasn't far behind them, and came out in that carry-chair, with Solamon and my friend Mr. Gilkie holding up the handles.

Now, I could go on here for another hour or so, telling you folks about the details. How we rounded up old Dills's bandits and held 'em in a stockade till we could turn them over to the military from Fort Davis. But heck! It'd just be some more of what you've already heard.

Both Dills and Silas Gresham stood trial for conspiracy, murder, and some other charges. They were found guilty and sentenced to hang. They appealed, of course, even though it ain't usually allowed after a military trial. Some outfit back in Washington City struck down that death penalty and sent them to the penitentiary at Fort Leavenworth to serve twenty years.

Dills's men were given a choice—either enlist for four years in the Regular Army or spend the same amount of time in prison. You can bet your last peso that they all joined up. Marshal Chidden's badge was taken away from him, and he narrowly missed going to jail. He left these parts and was never missed. Rush was offered the job but turned it down.

Solamon was given a hearing and was turned loose, 'cause he'd helped us beat that bunch. He decided to stay here in Texas and has a small place down the road a ways.

Old Justice McCowan was nursed by Maw till his wound was healed, then he 'n' Trace left for Montana Territory. Mahlon, he hung around for a few days, then went back east. I hear he's a lawyer now, and doing just fine.

The real storybook ending came when my maw drove up the lane in a buckboard, with li'l old Samuel Walker Wyeth hanging on to the reins, and Julia in back, a baby in her arms.

Old Rush, he hemmed and hawed and pawed the ground, but he finally went on over there and gave her a big kiss. Her face lit up like all get-out, and she kissed him back, with a big hug to boot! We all crowded around to see the baby, and old Milo, he was proud as punch. It was a boy child, of course. Us McCowans, we run mostly to boys, it seems. Them Choctaws, they all come in close, and Handsome Horse insisted on holding the baby. He hoisted him up in the air, turning to face the sun, and named him Toba-patakitta, which was Choctaw for "Born of a Brave," Brave meaning warrior.

So you see, everything turned out just fine. Taken a while for the fuss to die down, then Milo mentioned he might buy drinks for the whole bunch next time we was all in town together, and there was a regular stampede for the horses.

About the
Author

A true Westerner by birth, Robert Vaughn Bell grew up
in the Nebraska cattle country. Bell has written exten-
sively about the Old West in magazine and newspaper ar-
ticles and in his previous four Western novels, all
published by Ballantine. He and his wife, Billie, reside
on their Creek Park Ranch, high in the foothills of the
California Sierras, where they raise beef cattle and continue research for his books.

GREAT TALES from the OLD WEST

OWEN ROUNTREE